THE RISE OF THE DIGITAL CRA

Jeff A. Parke

Transforming Clinical Research in the Digital Age: A Comprehensive Guide for Clinical Research Associates

From Paper to Pixels: How the Digital CRA Is Revolutionizing Clinical Research

Objectives of the book:

The rise of artificial intelligence (AI), digital CRAs, and machine learning is transforming the field of clinical research in profound ways. This eBook provides a comprehensive guide to these cutting-edge technologies, giving CRAs the tools and knowledge they need to stay ahead of the curve.

AI is revolutionizing clinical trial operations by enabling faster and more accurate data analysis. Machine learning algorithms can sift through vast amounts of data and identify patterns and insights that may be missed by human analysts. This can lead to faster drug development and improved patient outcomes.

Digital CRAs are also playing an increasingly important role in clinical trials. These professionals use advanced digital tools to monitor and manage trials remotely, reducing the need for on-site visits and improving efficiency. This is particularly important in light of the COVID-19 pandemic, which has made remote monitoring essential for many trials.

In addition, machine learning algorithms are being used to predict patient outcomes and identify potential safety issues. By analyzing patient data in real-time, these algorithms can alert researchers to potential problems before they become serious.

Overall, the rise of AI, digital CRAs, and machine learning is transforming the field of clinical research, offering new opportunities for innovation and improved patient outcomes. By mastering these technologies, CRAs can stay ahead of the curve and make a meaningful impact in the world of clinical research.

Introduction:

Clinical research has come a long way since its inception, and the introduction of artificial intelligence (AI), machine learning (ML), and natural language processing (NLP) has brought about a significant transformation in the Clinical Research Associate (CRA) landscape. With the increasing complexity and volume of clinical data, the traditional manual approach to data management is no longer efficient.

The introduction of AI has opened up new avenues for capturing, managing, and disseminating data through data capture systems and electronic data vaults. The use of AI and other emerging technologies is revolutionizing the way CRAs work with community-based sites, private practices, and academic centers. With the ability to analyze vast amounts of data in real-time, AI provides CRAs with valuable insights into patient recruitment, site selection, and monitoring, ultimately leading to more efficient and effective clinical trial management.

Transforming Clinical Research in the Digital Age: A Comprehensive Guide for Clinical Research Associates is an eBook that provides a comprehensive look at the role of CRAs in clinical trials. This guide recognizes the importance of incorporating AI into the clinical trial process and discusses its potential impact on clinical research. As we move forward, the integration of AI and other emerging technologies will be vital for the success of clinical trials, and this guide aims to equip CRAs with the knowledge and tools needed to adapt to these changes and remain at the forefront of clinical research.

Clinical research associates (CRAs) are unsung heroes in the field of medical research, ensuring that clinical trials are conducted safely and ethically. They play a critical role in bringing new treatments and therapies to market, and ultimately improving patient outcomes. However, the work of CRAs goes beyond just conducting clinical trials. They are also community advocates, working to ensure that clinical trials are accessible and inclusive for patients from all backgrounds and communities.

This comprehensive guide to community reinvestment and development is a call to action for all CRAs and those aspiring to enter the field. We will explore the essential role that CRAs play in clinical trials, as well as their broader impact on the community. From site management and co-monitoring to site selection and the integration of AI technology, we will delve into every aspect of CRA work.

But more than that, this book is a reminder of the vital importance of community reinvestment in clinical research. We will examine how CRAs can work to ensure that clinical trials are conducted ethically and inclusively, benefiting the communities in which they take place. We will explore the challenges that CRAs face in their work, including navigating complex regulations and ensuring compliance with ethical guidelines.

Through real-world case studies and examples, we will highlight the impact that CRAs can have on patient outcomes and community service. We will also examine the critical role that AI technology plays in clinical trial operations, and the ethical and regulatory considerations that must be considered when using AI.

Chapter 1: Understanding the Role of CRAs in Clinical Trials

Clinical trials are the backbone of medical research, ensuring that new treatments and therapies are safe and effective for patients. Conducting clinical trials involves a complex web of activities, from recruiting participants to collecting and analyzing data. One critical role in this process is that of the clinical research associate (CRA).

CRAs are responsible for overseeing the day-to-day operations of clinical trials, ensuring that they are conducted safely and ethically. They work closely with investigators and study coordinators to monitor the progress of the trial and ensure that it adheres to the study protocol.The role of CRAs has evolved significantly over the years, as clinical trials have become more complex and heavily regulated. In the early days of clinical research, CRAs primarily focused on data entry and verification. Today, however, they play a much more critical role in the overall success of clinical trials.

One key area in which CRAs have made a significant impact is in participant recruitment and retention. Clinical trials are often conducted with a specific patient population in mind, and recruiting and retaining participants from that population can be challenging. CRAs work with study sites to identify potential participants, educate them about the study, and ensure that they receive appropriate care throughout the trial.

Furthermore, CRAs play a crucial role in ensuring that clinical trials are conducted in an ethical and inclusive manner. They work to ensure that study sites have appropriate policies and procedures in place to protect the rights and welfare of study participants. They also ensure that studies are conducted in compliance with all applicable regulations and guidelines, including the Declaration of Helsinki, Good Clinical Practice (GCP), and local laws and regulations.

The importance of CRAs in clinical trials cannot be overstated. They are the guardians of patient safety and ethical research practices. Without their expertise and dedication, clinical trials would not be possible.

Real-World Case Study:

A pharmaceutical company was conducting a clinical trial to test a new treatment for a rare genetic disorder. The study population was limited to patients with the disorder, which made recruitment and retention challenging. The study was in danger of falling behind schedule, and the pharmaceutical company was considering canceling the trial.

Enter the CRAs. They worked with study sites to identify potential participants, educate them about the study, and ensure that they received appropriate care throughout the trial. They also worked with the pharmaceutical company to develop new recruitment strategies, including outreach to patient advocacy groups and social media campaigns.

Thanks to the efforts of the CRAs, the study was able to recruit and retain enough participants to complete the trial successfully. The treatment was ultimately approved by regulatory authorities and is now available to patients with the disorder. This case study demonstrates the critical role that CRAs play in the success of clinical trials.

Table 1: Key Responsibilities of CRAs in Clinical Trials

Responsibility	**Description**
Study Monitoring	Ensuring that the study is conducted in accordance with the protocol and Good Clinical Practice (GCP) guidelines
Site Management	Managing study sites, including ensuring that they have appropriate policies and procedures in place
Participant Recruitment and Retention	Identifying potential participants and ensuring that they receive appropriate care throughout the trial
Data Management	Ensuring the accuracy and completeness of study data
Quality Assurance	Conducting internal audits to ensure compliance with regulatory and

Responsibility	Description
	ethical guidelines
Compliance	Ensuring that the study is conducted in compliance with all applicable regulations and guidelines

CRAs play a pivotal role in the success of clinical trials. They are the guardians of patient safety and ethical research practices. They work tirelessly to ensure that studies are conducted in an ethical and inclusive manner, benefiting patients and communities around the world. In the next chapter, we will delve into the critical

Chapter 2: Site Selection Techniques in Clinical Trials

Site selection is a critical aspect of clinical trial management. The success of a clinical trial depends on the selection of appropriate sites and investigators. The process of site selection involves identifying potential sites and investigators, evaluating their qualifications and experience, and selecting the best candidates for the study.However, the limitations of traditional randomized controlled trials (RCTs) are increasingly being recognized, including their limited generalizability to real-world patients and settings. This is where real-world data (RWD) and real-world evidence (RWE) come into play.

Real-world data are generated from various sources, including electronic health records (EHRs), claims databases, and patient registries. They provide a comprehensive view of patients' health status, treatment patterns, and outcomes in routine clinical practice. Real-world evidence, on the other hand, refers to the use of RWD to support clinical and regulatory decision-making.

The use of RWE in clinical trials has many benefits. First and foremost, it can help address some of the limitations of traditional RCTs, such as narrow patient populations, strict eligibility criteria, and limited follow-up periods. RWE can provide a broader representation of patients in routine clinical practice, including those with comorbidities, older age, and more diverse racial and ethnic backgrounds. This can enhance the generalizability and relevance of clinical trial findings to real-world patients and settings.

In addition, RWE can help accelerate the drug development process by providing valuable insights into the safety and efficacy of new treatments in routine clinical practice. It can also support post-marketing surveillance and monitoring of drug safety and effectiveness.

Several initiatives have been launched to promote the use of RWE in clinical research. For example, the FDA's Real-World Evidence Program aims to facilitate the use of RWE to support regulatory decision-making. The Observational Medical Outcomes Partnership (OMOP) is another initiative that aims to develop and validate methods for analyzing RWD to generate RWE.

Real-world evidence can also be used to support community service and community engagement. By including diverse populations and patient groups in clinical trials and using RWE to understand the unique needs of these groups, researchers can develop interventions and treatment strategies that better serve the needs of these communities.

Real-world data and evidence are a powerful tool for clinical research, and their use is becoming increasingly important in the development of new treatments and interventions. However, it is important to ensure that the data used are of high quality and reliable, and that appropriate methods are used to analyze and interpret the data.This data is collected through various means such as electronic health records (EHRs), claims databases, patient registries, and other sources. The role of the CRA in RWE is to ensure that data is collected in a standardized and consistent manner, adhering to regulatory guidelines and industry best practices.

The CRA is responsible for monitoring and overseeing the data collection process at the site level. They ensure that the data is accurate, complete, and of high quality. They also ensure that the data is collected in a timely manner and that the study protocol is being followed. This is important because the quality of the data collected can impact the validity and reliability of the study results.
Proper site selection is also critical in RWE studies. The CRA plays a crucial role in this process as well. They work with the study team to identify potential sites for the study based on various criteria such as patient population, availability of data sources, and geographic location. The CRA also conducts site assessments to ensure that the site has the necessary resources, personnel, and infrastructure to conduct the study.

In addition to the CRA's role in site selection and data collection, RWE is also important for post-market surveillance and safety monitoring. RWE studies can provide valuable information on the safety and effectiveness of a drug or medical device once it has been approved for use. This information can be used by regulatory agencies to make informed decisions about the use of the product.

To illustrate the importance of RWE in site selection, let's consider a case study. Imagine a pharmaceutical company is developing a new drug for the treatment of a rare disease. To conduct a clinical trial, the company needs to identify sites with a sufficient number of patients with the disease. However, because the disease is rare, it may be difficult to identify sites that meet this criteria.

By leveraging RWE, the company can identify sites that have a high prevalence of the disease based on EHRs, claims databases, and patient registries. This information can then be used to select sites for the clinical trial. The CRA can then work with the selected sites to ensure that the data is collected in a standardized and consistent manner, ensuring the validity and reliability of the study results.

The CRA plays an intricate role in RWE, from site selection to data collection and analysis. RWE is vital for proper site selection and can provide valuable information for post-market surveillance and safety monitoring. By leveraging RWE, pharmaceutical companies and researchers can make informed decisions about the use of drugs and medical devices, ultimately improving patient outcomes.

Chapter 3: Co-Monitoring Visits in Clinical Trials

Co-monitoring visits (CMVs) are an essential component of clinical trials. They involve a clinical research associate (CRA) and a clinical investigator visiting the trial site together to review the accuracy and completeness of data and ensure protocol compliance. CMVs play a critical role in ensuring data integrity and preventing fraud and misconduct in clinical trials.

During a CMV, the CRA provides guidance and feedback to the investigator and site staff, reviews the site's adherence to the protocol, and identifies any potential problems. The visit is an opportunity for the CRA and investigator to discuss any issues or concerns that may arise during the study and develop a plan to mitigate them. By conducting CMVs, CRAs can help ensure that the study is being conducted in compliance with the protocol and that data is being collected accurately and completely.

CMVs are typically conducted when a CRA is in training or shadowing an experienced CRA. The purpose of these visits is to provide the trainee with hands-on experience and guidance from an experienced CRA while also ensuring that the study is being conducted in compliance with the protocol. The trainee may take on certain responsibilities during the visit, such as reviewing source documents or case report forms (CRFs), under the supervision of the experienced CRA.

The CRA assesses the investigator's training needs and provides guidance and support to ensure that they have all the necessary resources to carry out the study. This may include providing training on the study protocol, ensuring that the investigator has access to all necessary study materials, and answering any questions or concerns the investigator may have. By providing this support, CRAs can help ensure that investigators are fully prepared to carry out the study and collect data accurately and completely.

During a CMV, the CRA and investigator work together to identify any potential problems and develop a plan to mitigate them. This may include identifying areas where the investigator or site staff may need additional training or support, addressing issues with data collection or documentation, or identifying potential sources of bias or error in the study. By identifying and addressing these issues early on, CRAs can help ensure that the study is conducted in compliance with the protocol and that data integrity is maintained throughout the study.

In addition to ensuring data integrity and protocol compliance, CMVs also provide hands-on training and development for new CRAs. By shadowing an experienced CRA during a CMV, new CRAs can learn about best practices for conducting site visits, interacting with investigators and site staff, and identifying potential problems or issues. This hands-on training can help new CRAs develop the necessary skills and experience to carry out their roles effectively and ensure that studies are conducted in compliance with the protocol.

As clinical trials continue to evolve and become more complex, the importance of co-monitoring visits in ensuring study quality and compliance cannot be overstated. By conducting regular CMVs, CRAs can help ensure that studies are conducted in compliance with the protocol, that data is collected accurately and completely, and that potential sources of bias or error are identified and addressed early on. Ultimately, this can lead to better patient outcomes and advancements in medical research.

Artificial intelligence (AI) and natural language processing (NLP) are rapidly advancing technologies that have the potential to revolutionize the way clinical trials are conducted, including co-monitoring visits (CMVs) and monitoring visits. These technologies can help improve the efficiency and accuracy of data collection, automate routine tasks, and identify potential issues and concerns early on in the study.

One way that AI and NLP can be used in CMVs is through automated data review. Rather than relying on manual review by a CRA, AI algorithms can be used to analyze and detect potential data errors or inconsistencies. This can help identify potential issues early in the study, allowing for quicker resolution and improved data quality. NLP can be used to analyze unstructured data such as medical notes and identify important information that may not be captured in structured data.

Another area where AI and NLP can be used in CMVs is in identifying potential risks and issues. By analyzing data from multiple sources, including electronic health records (EHRs), social media, and other sources, AI algorithms can identify potential safety concerns and adverse events. This can help CRAs, and investigators identify potential risks early on in the study and develop strategies to mitigate those risks.

AI and NLP can also be used to improve the efficiency of CMVs and monitoring visits. For example, AI algorithms can be used to prioritize which sites to visit based on risk and data quality, helping CRAs and investigators focus their efforts on sites where they are most needed. NLP can be used to automate certain tasks, such as identifying and categorizing adverse events, reducing the amount of time and effort required by CRAs and investigators.

AI and NLP can also be used to analyze data from multiple clinical trials, providing insights into trends and patterns that may not be immediately apparent from individual studies. This can help researchers identify potential risk factors, improve study design, and develop more effective treatments and interventions.

One potential application of AI and NLP in CMVs is in fraud and misconduct detection. AI algorithms can be trained to identify potential fraudulent behavior, such as data manipulation or falsification. By analyzing data from multiple sources and identifying patterns of behavior that may indicate fraud, AI can help identify potential issues early in the study and prevent fraud and misconduct from occurring.

However, there are also potential challenges and limitations to using AI and NLP in CMVs and monitoring visits. For example, AI algorithms may not be able to capture the nuances and complexities of human interaction and communication, which are critical components of CMVs and monitoring visits. Additionally, AI and NLP algorithms may be limited by the quality and quantity of data available, particularly in smaller or less well-funded studies.

Another potential limitation of AI and NLP is the potential for bias. AI algorithms are only as unbiased as the data they are trained on, and if the data is biased, the algorithm may produce biased results. Additionally, NLP algorithms may struggle with language barriers or non-standard terminology, particularly in multi-lingual studies.

Despite these potential challenges, the use of AI and NLP in CMVs and monitoring visits has the potential to significantly improve the efficiency and effectiveness of clinical trials. By automating routine tasks, identifying potential risks and issues, and improving data quality and accuracy, AI and NLP can help ensure that studies are conducted in compliance with the protocol and that data integrity is maintained throughout the study.

While AI and NLP are still emerging technologies, they have the potential to significantly improve the way clinical trials are conducted, including co-monitoring visits and monitoring visits. As these technologies continue to evolve and mature, it is likely that they will become an increasingly important component of clinical trial management, helping to improve patient outcomes and advance medical research.

Chapter 4: Site Management in Clinical Trials

One of the primary responsibilities of site management is to ensure that the site is adequately trained. This includes training on the study protocol, study procedures, and any required documentation. The site manager should also ensure that all staff members are aware of their roles and responsibilities and that they understand the importance of data quality and integrity.

Site management also involves ensuring that the site is adhering to the study timeline and that all required documentation is completed and submitted on time. The site manager should also ensure that any deviations from the protocol are reported and documented appropriately.

Another critical aspect of site management is ensuring that the site is adequately equipped. This includes ensuring that all equipment and supplies are available, and that they are in good working order. The site manager should also ensure that all study drugs are stored and dispensed appropriately, and that any adverse events or serious adverse events are reported promptly.

Site management involves several key activities, including site selection, site initiation, ongoing site training and support, and site closeout. Site selection is a crucial first step in site management, as it involves identifying and evaluating potential study sites based on specific criteria, such as the availability of eligible patients, the experience and qualifications of the site staff, and the site's track record in conducting similar studies.

Once the site is selected, site initiation involves ensuring that the site is adequately prepared to conduct the study. This includes providing the site staff with training on the study protocol, the study drug or device, and any specific procedures or assessments required for the study. The study team also needs to ensure that the site has all the necessary equipment, supplies, and resources to conduct the study.

Ongoing site training and support are crucial to ensure that the site remains compliant with the study protocol and applicable regulations throughout the study. This involves regular communication and feedback between the study team and the site staff, as well as monitoring of site performance and data quality.

Site management is a critical component of clinical trials. It involves coordinating and managing activities at the trial site, including recruitment, data collection, and protocol adherence. Effective site management is essential to ensure that the study is conducted in compliance with the protocol and that data integrity is maintained throughout the study. However, site management can be complex and time-consuming, and traditional methods may not always be sufficient to ensure optimal outcomes. Real-world evidence (RWE) and artificial intelligence (AI) have the potential to support improved site management in clinical trials, providing valuable insights and streamlining processes.

RWE refers to data collected outside of a traditional clinical trial setting, such as electronic health records, claims data, and patient-generated data. RWE can provide a wealth of information that can help improve site management in clinical trials. For example, RWE can be used to identify potential study participants based on demographic and clinical characteristics. This can help improve recruitment efforts and ensure that the study includes a diverse population. Additionally, RWE can be used to identify potential barriers to recruitment, such as lack of awareness or access to study sites and help develop strategies to address those barriers.

RWE can also be used to improve the efficiency of site management. For example, by analyzing data from multiple sources, RWE can identify potential issues and concerns early in the study, allowing for quicker resolution and improved data quality. Additionally, RWE can be used to monitor patient outcomes and identify potential adverse events, allowing for early intervention and improved patient safety.

AI is another technology that can support improved site management in clinical trials. AI algorithms can be used to analyze data from multiple sources, identify potential risks and issues, and provide insights into patient outcomes and study efficacy. For example, AI algorithms can be used to analyze data from electronic health records and identify potential participants for the study based on clinical characteristics. Additionally, AI can be used to analyze data from patient-reported outcomes and identify trends or patterns that may be missed through traditional data analysis.

AI can also be used to streamline site management processes. For example, AI algorithms can be used to prioritize which sites to visit based on risk and data quality, helping CRAs and investigators focus their efforts on sites where they are most needed. Additionally, AI can be used to automate certain tasks, such as identifying and categorizing adverse events, reducing the amount of time and effort required by CRAs and investigators.

One potential application of RWE and AI in site management is patient engagement. By leveraging patient-generated data, such as wearable device data or social media activity, researchers can gain valuable insights into patient behavior and preferences. This information can be used to design more effective recruitment strategies, develop patient-centered study designs, and improve patient retention and engagement throughout the study.

Another potential application of RWE and AI in site management is in data quality and integrity. By analyzing data from multiple sources and identifying potential issues and concerns early in the study, RWE and AI can help ensure that the study is conducted in compliance with the protocol and that data integrity is maintained throughout the study. Additionally, RWE and AI can be used to identify potential fraud and misconduct, helping to ensure that the study is conducted ethically and with the highest level of integrity.

Despite the potential benefits of RWE and AI in site management, there are also potential challenges and limitations. For example, RWE may be limited by the quality and quantity of data available, particularly in smaller or less well-funded studies. Additionally, AI algorithms may not be able to capture the nuances and complexities of human interaction and communication, which are critical components of site management.

Another potential challenge is the need for adequate training and support for CRAs and investigators. As RWE and AI become more integrated into site management processes, it is important to ensure that CRAs and investigators have the AI and RWE can also support improved site management in clinical trials by providing real-time monitoring and analysis of site performance. By using machine learning algorithms, AI can analyze data from multiple sources to identify patterns and trends in site performance, enabling site managers to make data-driven decisions. For example, AI can analyze data on patient recruitment rates, enrollment timelines, and protocol compliance to identify potential issues and provide recommendations for improvement.

RWE can also provide valuable insights into site performance. Real-world data can be collected from various sources, such as electronic health records, claims data, and patient registries, to provide a comprehensive view of patient populations and treatment outcomes. This data can be used to identify patient populations that may be suitable for clinical trials, as well as to inform study design and endpoint selection. Additionally, RWE can be used to monitor site performance, such as patient recruitment rates and protocol compliance, providing valuable feedback to site managers and enabling them to make informed decisions about site operations.

In addition to monitoring site performance, AI and RWE can also support site management by improving communication and collaboration between site staff and study teams. AI-powered chatbots and virtual assistants can provide 24/7 support to site staff, answering common questions and providing guidance on study procedures and protocols. This can help to improve efficiency and reduce errors, as site staff can quickly access information and support when needed. Furthermore, AI can facilitate real-time collaboration between site staff and study teams, enabling them to share information and collaborate on study-related tasks in a secure and efficient manner.

RWE can also facilitate communication and collaboration between site staff and study teams. Real-world data can be shared between study teams and site staff to inform study design and endpoint selection, as well as to provide feedback on site performance. Furthermore, RWE can be used to support patient engagement and retention, by providing insights into patient preferences and behavior. This can help to improve patient satisfaction and reduce the risk of dropout, ultimately improving the quality of clinical trial data.

Overall, AI and RWE have the potential to revolutionize site management in clinical trials, by providing real-time monitoring and analysis of site performance, improving communication and collaboration between site staff and study teams, and supporting patient engagement and retention. By harnessing the power of these technologies, site managers can make data-driven decisions, improve study efficiency, and ultimately enhance the quality of clinical trial data.

Chapter 5 Site close

During the site close-out visit, the CRA confirms that all study-related activities have been completed, including the collection of all necessary data and specimens. The CRA also ensures that the site has properly stored and maintained all study-related documents and records. The CRA also verifies that the site has appropriately disposed of any unused study drugs or materials.

In addition, the CRA conducts an audit of the site's records to ensure that the study has been conducted in compliance with the study protocol, regulatory requirements, and industry best practices. Any deviations from the study protocol are documented and reported to the study team.
Now moving onto the chapter on site selection techniques, it is important to consider several factors when selecting sites for a clinical trial. These factors include the patient population, availability of data sources, geographic location, and the site's infrastructure and resources.

To determine the patient population, the CRA may work with the study team to identify potential sites based on the prevalence of the disease or condition being studied. They may also consider the demographics of the patient population and whether the site has access to a diverse patient population.

Availability of data sources is another important consideration. The CRA may look at electronic health records, claims databases, and patient registries to determine whether the site has access to the necessary data sources. This is particularly important for RWE studies, as discussed earlier. Geographic location is also important. The CRA may consider the proximity of the site to the study team, as well as the ease of patient recruitment and retention. The CRA may also consider any potential logistical challenges, such as transportation or language barriers.

Finally, the site's infrastructure and resources are critical considerations. The CRA may assess the site's personnel, equipment, and facilities to determine whether they have the necessary resources to conduct the study. The CRA may also consider the site's experience with clinical trials and their track record of meeting study timelines and requirements.

Site selection is a complex process that requires careful consideration of several factors. The CRA plays a critical role in this process, working with the study team to identify potential sites and conducting site assessments to ensure that the site has the necessary resources to conduct the study. Site close-out visits are also important to ensure that the study has been conducted in compliance with the study protocol and regulatory requirements.

Table: Example of a Potential Site List

Site Name	Patient Population	Data Sources	Geographic Location	Infrastructure and Resources
Site A	High prevalence of disease	Access to EHRs and patient registries	Urban area with good transportation	Experienced staff, well-equipped facilities
Site B	Diverse patient population	Access to claims databases	Rural area with limited transportation	Limited staff, basic equipment and facilities
Site C	Moderate prevalence of disease	Access to all data sources	Suburban area with moderate transportation	Experienced staff, well-equipped facilities

This table could be used to compare potential sites based on several key factors, including patient population, data sources, geographic location, and infrastructure and resources.

Chapter 9: The Future of Clinical Trials and Site Management

Clinical trials are complex and resource-intensive processes that involve numerous stakeholders, including sponsors, investigators, and study participants. Over the years, the traditional clinical trial site management system has undergone significant changes. Emerging trends in clinical trial site management include the adoption of innovative technologies, patient-centric approaches, and the use of real-world data. These trends are expected to revolutionize the way clinical trials are conducted in the future.

The potential impact of new technologies on site management is significant. Technologies such as electronic health records (EHRs), telemedicine, and mobile health (mHealth) devices can help improve patient recruitment, reduce trial timelines, and increase the quality of data collected. Moreover, the use of wearables and sensors can help researchers collect real-time patient data, enabling them to monitor patient health and safety more effectively.

To build a more efficient and effective clinical trial site management system, stakeholders need to adopt strategies that address the challenges faced in traditional site management. These strategies should focus on the following areas:

1. Patient recruitment and retention: The use of innovative technologies and patient-centric approaches can help improve patient recruitment and retention.
2. Protocol design and optimization: Optimizing study protocols can help reduce timelines and minimize the need for protocol amendments.
3. Data management: The use of centralized data management systems can help improve data quality and reduce the time and resources required for data cleaning.
4. Risk management: Implementing risk-based monitoring strategies can help reduce the need for on-site monitoring visits and increase the focus on critical data points.

Chapter 10: Introduction to Artificial Intelligence (AI) in Clinical Trials

Artificial Intelligence (AI) has the potential to transform clinical trials by enabling researchers to make more informed decisions and improve patient outcomes. The use of AI in clinical trials is expected to revolutionize the way trials are designed, conducted, and analyzed.

The impact of AI on clinical trials is significant, with benefits ranging from improved patient safety and recruitment to enhanced data analysis and decision-making. AI can help automate many aspects of clinical trial operations, including patient screening, data collection, and analysis. Additionally, AI can identify potential safety issues and enable researchers to intervene before adverse events occur.

Despite its potential benefits, the use of AI in clinical trials also poses challenges and limitations. One significant challenge is the lack of regulatory guidelines for AI in clinical trials. Additionally, the integration of AI-based technologies into existing clinical trial operations requires significant investment in infrastructure and personnel training.

The role of Clinical Research Associates (CRAs) in implementing AI technology in clinical trials is crucial. CRAs can help ensure that AI-based technologies are integrated seamlessly into clinical trial operations, and that data is accurately collected and analyzed. Moreover, CRAs can monitor patient safety and compliance with study protocols to identify potential issues early on.

Chapter 11: Revolutionizing Clinical Trials: The Critical Role of CRAs in AI-Based Data Management and Compliance

Clinical research associates (CRAs) play a critical role in ensuring the accuracy and completeness of data in clinical trials. However, with the increasing amount of data generated during clinical trials, managing, and monitoring it has become a challenging task. This is where artificial intelligence (AI) comes in. AI-based data management in clinical trials offers numerous benefits, from increased efficiency and accuracy to improved compliance with regulatory requirements.

11.1 Importance of data management in clinical trials

Effective data management is crucial for the success of clinical trials. Accurate and complete data is required to ensure that the results are reliable and can be used to make informed decisions about the safety and efficacy of a drug or medical device. In addition, regulatory agencies require that data be collected and managed in a manner that complies with their guidelines. Failure to comply with these guidelines can result in significant fines or even the suspension of clinical trials.

11.2 Benefits of using AI for data management in clinical trials

The use of AI in data management for clinical trials has numerous benefits. One of the primary benefits is increased efficiency. AI can automate many of the manual tasks associated with data management, such as data cleaning and quality control, freeing up CRAs to focus on more complex tasks. In addition, AI can improve the accuracy of data by identifying and correcting errors in real-time. This can help to ensure that the data collected during clinical trials is reliable and of high quality.

Another benefit of using AI in data management is improved compliance with regulatory requirements. AI can help to ensure that data is collected, managed, and reported in a manner that complies with regulatory guidelines. This can help to reduce the risk of fines or other penalties for non-compliance.

11.3 Role of CRAs in ensuring data accuracy and completeness

Despite the benefits of AI in data management, CRAs still play a critical role in ensuring the accuracy and completeness of data in clinical trials. While AI can automate many tasks, there are still aspects of data management that require human expertise and judgment. CRAs are responsible for ensuring that the data collected during clinical trials is accurate and complete. They must also ensure that the data is entered into the system correctly, and that any errors or discrepancies are identified and corrected.

11.4 Strategies for effective AI-based data management in clinical trials

To ensure effective AI-based data management in clinical trials, there are several strategies that CRAs can employ. One strategy is to ensure that the AI system is properly trained and validated. This involves testing the system to ensure that it is accurate and reliable. Another strategy is to ensure that the data being collected is of high quality. This can be achieved by using standardized data collection methods and ensuring that the data is entered into the system correctly.

In addition, CRAs should ensure that the data management process is transparent and auditable. This can be achieved by documenting all data management activities and ensuring that they are traceable back to the source data. Finally, it is important to ensure that the AI system is integrated with the overall clinical trial management system. This can help to ensure that data is managed in a coordinated and efficient manner, and that any issues or discrepancies are identified and addressed in a timely manner.

AI-based data management in clinical trials offers numerous benefits, from increased efficiency and accuracy to improved compliance with regulatory requirements. However, CRAs still play a critical role in ensuring the accuracy and completeness of data in clinical trials. By employing effective strategies for AI-based data management, CRAs can help to ensure that clinical trials are conducted in a manner that is compliant with regulatory requirements and that produces reliable and high-quality data.

Chapter 12: AI-Based Compliance Monitoring in Clinical Trials

In any clinical trial, maintaining regulatory compliance is critical to ensure the safety and well-being of study participants. Traditional methods of compliance monitoring involve manual checks, which can be time-consuming, prone to errors, and limited in scope. However, the advent of AI-based technologies has opened new possibilities for more efficient and effective compliance monitoring.

One of the main advantages of using AI for compliance monitoring is its ability to analyze large volumes of data in real-time. Machine learning algorithms can be trained to identify patterns and anomalies in data that may indicate non-compliance, such as deviations from the study protocol or adverse events. This allows CRAs to take proactive measures to address potential compliance issues before they become major problems.

Another benefit of AI-based compliance monitoring is its ability to provide more accurate and reliable data. By automating compliance checks, AI technology eliminates the potential for human error and ensures that data is recorded consistently and accurately. This not only improves the quality of data collected but also saves time and resources by reducing the need for manual data entry and validation.

However, there are also potential challenges and limitations associated with the use of AI for compliance monitoring. One major concern is the risk of bias in AI algorithms, which can result in false positives or negatives that could have serious consequences for study participants. Additionally, the use of AI technology may raise ethical and regulatory concerns that must be addressed to ensure the integrity and safety of clinical trial data.

To address these challenges, CRAs must take an active role in implementing AI-based compliance monitoring systems. This includes ensuring that AI algorithms are rigorously tested and validated to minimize the risk of bias and errors. CRAs must also work closely with regulatory bodies to ensure that AI-based compliance monitoring systems meet all ethical and regulatory requirements.

Case study: A large pharmaceutical company was conducting a phase III clinical trial for a new drug designed to treat a rare genetic disorder. The study involved over 500 participants across multiple sites in different countries, making compliance monitoring a complex and challenging task. To address this challenge, the company implemented an AI-based compliance monitoring system that used machine learning algorithms to analyze data from electronic health records, laboratory results, and other sources. The system was able to identify potential compliance issues in real-time, allowing CRAs to take prompt action to address any deviations from the study protocol. As a result, the trial was completed on schedule and with a high level of data accuracy and regulatory compliance.

Chapter 13: The Future of AI in Clinical Trials

As AI technology continues to evolve, there is growing interest in its potential applications in clinical trials. Emerging trends in AI technology are expected to have a significant impact on clinical trial operations, including site management, compliance monitoring, and data management.

One key trend is the increasing use of natural language processing (NLP) to extract data from unstructured sources such as electronic health records, physician notes, and patient diaries. NLP technology uses machine learning algorithms to identify and extract relevant data from text, allowing CRAs to gain insights into study participants' experiences and improve data accuracy and completeness.

Another emerging trend is the use of AI-powered virtual assistants to automate routine tasks and improve communication and collaboration between study stakeholders. Virtual assistants can be used to schedule appointments, track study progress, and provide real-time feedback to study participants, improving engagement and retention in clinical trials.

AI technology is also expected to have a significant impact on the design and execution of clinical trials. Machine learning algorithms can be used to analyze historical data and identify potential risks and opportunities, allowing study designers to optimize study protocols and reduce the risk of failure.

However, as with any new technology, there are also potential challenges and limitations associated with the use of AI in clinical trials. These include ethical and regulatory concerns, as well as the need for specialized.

Chapter 14: Ethical and Regulatory Considerations in the Use of AI in Clinical Trials

AI technology has tremendous potential to revolutionize clinical trials, but it also raises significant ethical and regulatory concerns. As AI and machine learning algorithms continue to evolve, it is critical to ensure that they are used in a responsible and ethical manner. One of the key ethical considerations surrounding the use of AI in clinical trials is patient privacy. Clinical trials involve sensitive personal information, and it is essential to protect the privacy and confidentiality of participants.

To ensure patient privacy, CRAs must implement appropriate security measures to safeguard the data collected during a clinical trial. This includes ensuring that only authorized personnel have access to the data, and that the data is stored securely using encryption and other security measures. Additionally, CRAs must obtain informed consent from study participants, informing them about the types of data that will be collected and how it will be used. This will help to build trust with participants and ensure that their privacy is protected.

Another ethical consideration is the potential for AI algorithms to introduce bias into the clinical trial process. Bias can occur when algorithms are trained on biased data, or when the algorithms themselves are designed with inherent biases. This can result in unequal treatment of study participants based on factors such as race, gender, or socioeconomic status. To address this issue, CRAs must ensure that their AI algorithms are designed and trained in a way that is free from bias. They must also continually monitor and evaluate the algorithms to ensure that they are not inadvertently introducing bias into the clinical trial process.

Regulatory considerations are also a significant concern when it comes to the use of AI in clinical trials. AI algorithms must comply with all applicable regulations, including the International Council for Harmonisation of Technical Requirements for Pharmaceuticals for Human Use (ICH) guidelines and the regulations of the regulatory authorities in the countries where the clinical trial is being conducted. CRAs must ensure that their AI algorithms comply with these regulations and guidelines to avoid delays or complications during the clinical trial process.

One of the main challenges facing CRAs when implementing AI technology in clinical trials is the lack of clear regulatory guidelines. Regulatory agencies are still in the process of developing guidelines and regulations specific to the use of AI in clinical trials, and CRAs must stay up-to-date on these developments to ensure that they are in compliance with all applicable regulations. In addition, CRAs must work with regulatory agencies to establish standards for the development, testing, and implementation of AI algorithms in clinical trials.

Despite these challenges, the potential benefits of using AI in clinical trials are significant. AI algorithms can help to improve the accuracy and efficiency of clinical trial data collection and analysis, leading to faster and more reliable results. They can also help to identify potential safety concerns more quickly, allowing for earlier intervention and potentially improving patient outcomes. By working closely with regulatory agencies and implementing appropriate ethical and security measures, CRAs can harness the power of AI to improve the clinical trial process while maintaining patient safety and privacy.

Case Study: Using AI to Monitor Adverse Events in Clinical Trials

One example of the potential benefits of using AI in clinical trials is the use of AI algorithms to monitor adverse events. Adverse events are negative side effects that can occur as a result of a drug or medical treatment, and they are a critical factor in determining the safety and efficacy of a new treatment. In traditional clinical trials, adverse events are typically monitored by human reviewers who manually review patient records for any signs of negative side effects. However, this process can be time-consuming and prone to errors.

To address these issues, researchers at Stanford University developed an AI algorithm to monitor adverse events in clinical trials. The algorithm uses natural language processing and machine learning techniques to analyze patient records and identify potential adverse events. The algorithm was trained on a dataset of over 100,000 patient records,

Chapter 15: The Future Landscape of CRAs in the Community and Patient Centeredness

Clinical research associates (CRAs) play a critical role in the success of clinical trials. They are responsible for ensuring that studies are conducted in compliance with regulatory guidelines, protocol requirements, and good clinical practices. In recent years, there has been a growing interest in leveraging AI and machine learning (ML) technologies to improve the efficiency and effectiveness of CRA activities. One of the areas where AI and ML can have a significant impact is in the management of clinical trial sites.

Traditionally, CRAs have been responsible for managing multiple sites, each with their unique set of challenges and complexities. However, with the advent of AI and ML technologies, it is now possible to manage sites more efficiently and effectively. For example, natural language processing (NLP) algorithms can be used to analyze site visit reports and identify areas where additional support may be needed. Similarly, ML algorithms can be used to predict which sites are most likely to experience issues, allowing CRAs to proactively intervene and prevent problems from arising.

To better understand the potential benefits of AI and ML in site management, let's consider a case study. In a recent study, researchers used NLP algorithms to analyze site visit reports from 31 clinical trial sites. The algorithms were trained to identify specific phrases and keywords that indicated issues with study conduct, such as poor patient recruitment, data quality issues, and protocol deviations. The results of the analysis showed that the NLP algorithms were able to accurately identify issues in the vast majority of cases. This allowed the CRAs to proactively address the issues and prevent them from becoming more significant.

Looking ahead, it is likely that CRAs will continue to play a critical role in clinical trial management. However, the role of CRAs may evolve in response to advances in AI and ML technologies. For example, it is possible that CRAs may become more focused on overseeing the work of AI and ML algorithms rather than conducting site visits themselves. This would allow CRAs to devote more time to other important activities, such as building relationships with study investigators and ensuring patient safety.

Moreover, patient-centeredness is becoming increasingly important in the clinical trial industry, and CRAs have a crucial role to play in this area as well. With the help of AI and ML technologies, CRAs can identify ways to improve the patient experience and make clinical trials more accessible and patient friendly. For example, AI algorithms can be used to analyze patient feedback and identify areas where improvements can be made, such as reducing the time it takes for patients to complete study procedures or improving the clarity of study materials.

AI and ML technologies have the potential to revolutionize the way that CRAs manage clinical trial sites. By leveraging these technologies, CRAs can identify issues more quickly and efficiently, allowing them to take proactive steps to address them before they become more significant. Looking ahead, it is likely that the role of CRAs will evolve in response to these technological advances, with a greater emphasis on overseeing the work of AI and ML algorithms. Additionally, CRAs can use these technologies to improve patient-centeredness and make clinical trials more accessible and patient-friendly.

Table 1: Benefits of AI and ML in Clinical Trial Monitoring

Benefit	**Explanation**
Improved accuracy and completeness	AI and ML algorithms can identify and flag potential data discrepancies and errors
Faster data review and analysis	Automated analysis of large data sets can be performed quickly and efficiently
Real-time monitoring and alerts	AI algorithms can monitor clinical trial data in real-time and alert CRAs to issues

Benefit	Explanation
Reduced workload and cost for CRAs	Automated processes can reduce the workload and cost of clinical trial monitoring
Improved patient safety and data quality	Automated monitoring can identify potential safety concerns and data errors

Table 2: Challenges and Limitations of AI and ML in Clinical Trial Monitoring

Challenge or Limitation	Explanation
Lack of standardization in data formats	Data from different sources may have different formats, making it challenging for AI algorithms to process and analyze them
Limited ability to detect certain issues	Some issues may require human judgement and interpretation, such as detecting adverse events or subjective outcomes
Data privacy and security concerns	The use of AI and ML in clinical trial monitoring raises concerns around data privacy and security
Limited interpretability of algorithms	AI and ML algorithms can be difficult to interpret, making it challenging to understand how they arrived at certain

Challenge or Limitation	Explanation
	results

Table 3: Potential Future Landscape of CRAs in Community and Patient-Centered Clinical Trials

Future Landscape	Explanation
Greater focus on patient-centeredness	CRAs will need to prioritize patient needs and preferences when designing and conducting clinical trials. This may involve utilizing patient feedback and involving patients in trial design and conduct.
Increased use of AI and ML in trial monitoring	CRAs will need to become familiar with and adept at using AI and ML algorithms for clinical trial monitoring. This will require additional training and education on these technologies and their applications in clinical research.
Greater emphasis on community-based clinical trials	Clinical trials that are conducted in community settings are often more accessible and more representative of real-world populations. CRAs will need to build relationships with community organizations and health care providers to facilitate these trials.

Future Landscape	Explanation
Greater collaboration between stakeholders in clinical research	The complex nature of clinical research requires collaboration among a range of stakeholders, including patients, investigators, sponsors, and regulatory agencies. CRAs will need to develop and maintain relationships with all stakeholders involved in clinical trials.
Increased use of remote and virtual trial conduct and monitoring methods	The COVID-19 pandemic has accelerated the use of remote and virtual trial conduct and monitoring methods. CRAs will need to become proficient in using these methods and technologies, including telemedicine and virtual study visits.

In Chapter 15, it is important to note that the role of CRAs in clinical research is evolving and
will continue to do so as new technologies and approaches emerge. As the use of AI, ML, and NLP becomes more widespread in clinical research, CRAs will need to adapt and become proficient in using these technologies for data management, compliance monitoring, and trial conduct.

In the future, CRAs will need to prioritize patient-centeredness in their approach to clinical research, working closely with patients and community organizations to design and conduct trials that meet patient needs and preferences. They will also need to become familiar with and adept at using AI and ML algorithms for trial monitoring and data management, while also ensuring ethical and regulatory compliance.

To succeed in this rapidly evolving landscape, CRAs will need to stay up-to-date with new developments and technologies in clinical research, participate in ongoing training and education programs, and continuously improve their skills and knowledge. Additionally, they will need to be flexible and adaptable to changing circumstances and able to work effectively with a range of stakeholders in the clinical research community.

The role of CRAs in clinical research is crucial for ensuring the safety and efficacy of new treatments and therapies. As the field evolves and new technologies are introduced, CRAs will need to adapt and expand their skills and knowledge to effectively manage clinical trials and ensure that they are conducted in a patient-centered, ethical, and regulatory compliant manner. By embracing new technologies and approaches, and working collaboratively with patients, investigators, sponsors, and regulatory agencies, CRAs can continue to play a critical role in advancing the field of clinical research and improving patient outcomes.

Chapter 16 Precision Based Care, AI and the CRA

Clinical Research Associates (CRAs) play a critical role in precision-based care. Precision medicine is a healthcare approach that considers individual variability in genes, environment, and lifestyle to provide tailored medical treatments. The goal of precision medicine is to optimize patient outcomes and improve the quality of care by providing personalized treatment plans that are unique to each patient. AI is transforming the precision-based care model by enabling the analysis of vast amounts of data from multiple sources, providing real-time insights into patient health, and enabling healthcare providers to make more informed decisions.

CRAs are involved in precision-based care in several ways. One of the primary roles of CRAs is to oversee clinical trials, which are essential for the development of new precision medicine treatments. CRAs work closely with physicians, study coordinators, and patients to ensure that the clinical trial process is conducted ethically and safely. They are responsible for ensuring that clinical trials are designed to answer specific research questions, recruiting eligible patients, monitoring patient safety and well-being, and ensuring that the trial is conducted according to the highest ethical standards.

The use of AI in precision-based care is transforming the way CRAs work. With AI-powered analytics, CRAs can analyze vast amounts of data in real-time to identify trends and patterns that would be difficult to detect using traditional methods. AI can analyze data from electronic health records, medical images, and other sources to provide valuable insights into patient health. For example, AI can analyze genetic data to identify patients who are at higher risk of developing certain diseases or who may respond better to specific treatments.

AI is also transforming the way CRAs work with patients. AI-powered chatbots and virtual assistants can provide patients with personalized advice and guidance based on their individual health needs. These tools can help patients manage their health conditions, make informed decisions about their treatment options, and stay engaged with their healthcare providers. AI can also help healthcare providers monitor patients remotely, enabling them to provide more proactive care and intervene early if necessary.

In addition to clinical trials and patient care, CRAs are also involved in data management and regulatory compliance. The use of AI in data management is transforming the way clinical trial data is captured, managed, and analyzed. AI-powered data capture systems can automate the process of data entry, reducing the risk of errors and enabling faster data analysis. AI can also help CRAs identify potential issues with data quality and compliance, enabling them to take corrective action before problems arise.

The use of AI in precision-based care has the potential to transform healthcare delivery in several ways. One of the most significant benefits of AI is its ability to provide personalized treatment plans based on individual patient needs. By analyzing vast amounts of data from multiple sources, AI can provide healthcare providers with valuable insights into patient health, enabling them to provide more effective and efficient care. AI can also help healthcare providers identify patients who are at higher risk of developing certain health conditions, enabling them to provide more proactive care and intervene early if necessary.

Another benefit of AI in precision-based care is its ability to improve patient outcomes. By providing personalized treatment plans based on individual patient needs, healthcare providers can optimize patient outcomes and improve the quality of care. AI can also help healthcare providers identify patients who are at higher risk of developing complications or adverse reactions to certain treatments, enabling them to adjust treatment plans accordingly.

AI is also transforming the way healthcare providers interact with patients. AI-powered chatbots and virtual assistants can provide patients with personalized advice and guidance based on their individual health needs. These tools can help patients manage their health conditions, make informed decisions about their treatment options, and stay engaged with their healthcare providers. AI can also help healthcare providers monitor patients remotely, enabling them to provide more proactive care and intervene early if necessary.

Furthermore, AI is playing a significant role in improving the efficiency and accuracy of data analysis and interpretation. With the help of machine learning algorithms, AI can quickly identify patterns and relationships in large and complex data sets. This ability is particularly useful in precision-based care, where patients' individual genetic, environmental, and lifestyle factors are considered when developing treatment plans. AI can help identify which treatment options are likely to be most effective for individual patients based on their unique characteristics.

In addition to improving data analysis and interpretation, AI is also transforming the way CRAs work with community-based sites, private practices, and academic centers. For instance, AI-powered virtual assistants can automate many administrative tasks, freeing up CRAs to focus on more critical activities, such as patient recruitment and engagement. Virtual assistants can also assist with data entry and management, reducing the risk of errors and freeing up time for CRAs to spend on other tasks.

Moreover, AI is helping to enhance patient engagement and participation in clinical trials. With the help of natural language processing (NLP), AI-powered chatbots can interact with patients in real-time, answering their questions and providing support throughout the clinical trial process. NLP-powered chatbots can also provide personalized reminders to patients, such as when to take medication or attend appointments, improving adherence and reducing dropouts.

AI is also helping to improve the efficiency and accuracy of site selection and management in clinical trials. For instance, AI-powered algorithms can analyze a wide range of data points, including patient demographics, trial eligibility criteria, and site capabilities, to identify the most suitable trial sites. This approach can help ensure that clinical trials are conducted in locations where the patient population is diverse and representative, increasing the generalizability of study results.

The integration of AI technology into clinical trials is transforming the role of CRAs and the way precision-based care is delivered. AI is enhancing data capture, management, and dissemination, as well as improving patient engagement and participation in clinical trials. Furthermore, AI is streamlining site selection and management, reducing the risk of errors, and increasing the efficiency and accuracy of trial processes. As AI continues to evolve, it will undoubtedly play an increasingly critical role in the clinical trial process, supporting CRAs and researchers in their efforts to develop safe, effective, and personalized treatments for patients.

Chapter 17: Ethics in AI and Healthcare – The Role of the digitized CRA

As AI continues to transform the healthcare industry, it is important to consider the ethical implications of its use. AI has the potential to improve patient outcomes, increase efficiency, and reduce costs, but it also poses ethical challenges that must be addressed.

One ethical concern is the potential for AI to perpetuate and exacerbate existing healthcare disparities. If AI algorithms are trained on biased data or are not designed to account for social determinants of health, they may perpetuate existing disparities in access to healthcare and health outcomes. It is important to ensure that AI algorithms are designed and tested in a way that considers these factors to ensure that they do not worsen existing health inequities.

Another ethical concern is the potential for AI to compromise patient privacy and confidentiality. As AI systems collect and analyze vast amounts of personal health data, it is essential to ensure that this data is kept secure and is not accessed or used inappropriately. There is also a risk that AI systems could be hacked or manipulated, leading to breaches of patient privacy and confidentiality.

In addition, there is a concern about the accountability and transparency of AI systems. As AI algorithms become more complex and opaquer, it can be challenging to understand how they make decisions. This lack of transparency can make it difficult to hold AI systems accountable for their decisions, particularly in cases where these decisions have significant consequences for patients.

To address these ethical concerns, it is essential to establish ethical guidelines for the development and use of AI in healthcare. These guidelines should ensure that AI systems are designed and tested in a way that considers social determinants of health and that they do not perpetuate existing healthcare disparities. They should also ensure that patient privacy and confidentiality are protected, and that AI systems are transparent and accountable.

Furthermore, it is important to involve patients, healthcare providers, and other stakeholders in the development and implementation of AI systems in healthcare. This involvement can help ensure that AI systems are designed to meet the needs of patients and that they are used in a way that is consistent with ethical principles.

AI has the potential to transform healthcare in significant ways, but it also poses ethical challenges that must be addressed. It is essential to establish ethical guidelines for the development and use of AI in healthcare, to ensure that these systems are designed and used in a way that is consistent with ethical principles. It is also important to involve patients, healthcare providers, and other stakeholders in the development and implementation of AI systems to ensure that they meet the needs of patients and are used in a way that is consistent with ethical principles.

The term 'digital CRA' refers to a digital clinical research assistant, which is an AI-powered system that assists in the management and analysis of clinical trial data. The use of such systems can play an integral role in ensuring quality and ethical outcomes in clinical research.

> *"Digital CRAs have the potential to revolutionize the clinical research industry, by streamlining data collection and analysis and improving the overall participant experience." - Rachel Rath, Director of Product at Science 37*

One way in which digital CRAs can help ensure quality and ethical outcomes is using natural language processing (NLP) algorithms. NLP is a branch of AI that enables computers to understand and analyze human language. In the context of clinical research, NLP can be used to analyze large volumes of data, such as electronic health records and patient-reported outcomes.

By analyzing this data, digital CRAs can identify patterns and trends that might not be immediately apparent to human researchers. For example, NLP algorithms can be used to identify adverse events or drug interactions that might have been missed by human researchers.

Another way in which digital CRAs can help ensure quality and ethical outcomes is by using artificial intelligence (AI) algorithms to assist with the design of clinical trials. AI algorithms can be used to analyze patient data and identify patient populations that are most likely to respond to a particular treatment.

This can help researchers design more effective and efficient clinical trials, which can lead to faster development of new treatments and therapies. In addition, by identifying patient populations that are most likely to benefit from a particular treatment, researchers can reduce the risk of exposing patients to unnecessary risks or harm.

Overall, the use of digital CRAs in clinical research can help ensure quality and ethical outcomes by providing researchers with the tools and insights they need to design and execute effective clinical trials. By leveraging the power of AI and NLP, digital CRAs can help identify patterns and trends that might otherwise go unnoticed and assist researchers in designing studies that are more likely to produce meaningful and clinically relevant results.

Chapter 18 The Rise of the Digital CRA

Over the past few years, there has been a significant rise in the use of digital clinical research associates (CRAs) in the healthcare industry. Digital CRAs are AI-powered systems that assist in the management and analysis of clinical trial data. These systems have the potential to revolutionize clinical research by improving efficiency, reducing costs, and ensuring quality and ethical outcomes.

Section 1: Overview of Digital CRAs

Digital CRAs are a relatively new technology that is rapidly gaining traction in the healthcare industry. These systems are designed to assist with the management and analysis of clinical trial data, which can be a time-consuming and complex process. Digital CRAs use a range of AI-powered tools and techniques to analyze data, identify patterns and trends, and assist with the design and execution of clinical trials.

One of the key advantages of digital CRAs is their ability to analyze large volumes of data quickly and accurately. This is particularly important in clinical research, where researchers are often dealing with vast amounts of data from multiple sources. Digital CRAs use natural language processing (NLP) algorithms to analyze data from electronic health records, patient-reported outcomes, and other sources. By analyzing this data, digital CRAs can identify patterns and trends that might not be immediately apparent to human researchers.

Digital CRAs can also assist with the design and execution of clinical trials. AI algorithms can be used to analyze patient data and identify patient populations that are most likely to respond to a particular treatment. This can help researchers design more effective and efficient clinical trials, which can lead to faster development of new treatments and therapies.

Overall, the use of digital CRAs in clinical research has the potential to improve efficiency, reduce costs, and ensure quality and ethical outcomes. These systems are still in the early stages of development, but they are already showing promise in the healthcare industry.

Section 2: Advantages of Digital CRAs in Clinical Research

There are several advantages to using digital CRAs in clinical research. One of the most significant advantages is the ability of these systems to analyze large volumes of data quickly and accurately. This is particularly important in clinical research, where researchers are often dealing with vast amounts of data from multiple sources. By using NLP algorithms, digital CRAs can analyze data from electronic health records, patient-reported outcomes, and other sources to identify patterns and trends that might not be immediately apparent to human researchers.

Another advantage of digital CRAs is their ability to assist with the design and execution of clinical trials. AI algorithms can be used to analyze patient data and identify patient populations that are most likely to respond to a particular treatment. This can help researchers design more effective and efficient clinical trials, which can lead to faster development of new treatments and therapies.

In addition to these advantages, digital CRAs can also help ensure quality and ethical outcomes in clinical research. By using AI-powered tools and techniques, digital CRAs can help identify adverse events or drug interactions that might have been missed by human researchers. This can help ensure that clinical trials are conducted in a way that is consistent with ethical principles and that the safety of patients is protected.

Overall, the use of digital CRAs in clinical research has the potential to improve efficiency, reduce costs, and ensure quality and ethical outcomes. By leveraging the power of AI and NLP, digital CRAs can assist researchers in designing and executing more effective clinical trials and ensure that these trials are conducted in a way that is consistent with ethical principles.

Section 3: Future of Digital CRAs in Healthcare

The use of digital CRAs in clinical research is still in the early stages of development, but it is already showing significant promise. As these systems continue to evolve and improve, it is likely that they will become an increasingly important tool in the healthcare industry.

One area where digital CRAs could have a significant impact is in personalized medicine. In addition to improving the quality of data analysis, digital CRAs can also streamline the management of clinical trials. By automating repetitive tasks such as data entry and monitoring, digital CRAs can reduce the workload of human CRAs, allowing them to focus on more complex tasks that require human expertise and judgment. This can lead to increased efficiency and reduced costs, as well as improved patient safety and data quality.

Another advantage of digital CRAs is their ability to adapt to changing circumstances. Unlike human CRAs, who may be limited by their own biases and experiences, digital CRAs can be trained to recognize patterns and trends that might be missed by humans. This can help researchers identify potential issues with a study before they become major problems and can help them adjust their strategies in real time to improve outcomes.

Despite the potential benefits of digital CRAs, there are also some concerns about their use. One concern is the potential for AI algorithms to perpetuate existing biases and inequities in healthcare. If digital CRAs are trained on biased data or are not designed to consider social determinants of health, they may perpetuate existing disparities in access to healthcare and health outcomes. To address this concern, it is important to ensure that digital CRAs are designed and tested in a way that considers these factors, and that they do not worsen existing health inequities.

Another concern is the potential for digital CRAs to compromise patient privacy and confidentiality. As digital CRAs collect and analyze vast amounts of personal health data, it is essential to ensure that this data is kept secure and is not accessed or used inappropriately. There is also a risk that digital CRAs could be hacked or manipulated, leading to breaches of patient privacy and confidentiality.

> *"The integration of digital tools into clinical research has created new opportunities for CRAs to improve trial operations and patient engagement." - Craig Lipset, Advisor and Founder of Clinical Innovation Partners*

To address these concerns, it is essential to establish ethical guidelines for the development and use of digital CRAs in clinical research. These guidelines should ensure that digital CRAs are designed and tested in a way that considers social determinants of health and that they do not perpetuate existing healthcare disparities. They should also ensure that patient privacy and confidentiality are protected, and that digital CRAs are transparent and accountable.

The rise of digital CRAs represents a significant development in the field of clinical research. By leveraging the power of AI and automation, digital CRAs can improve the quality of data analysis, streamline the management of clinical trials, and adapt to changing circumstances in real time. However, it is important to address concerns about bias, privacy, and accountability to ensure that digital CRAs are used in a way that is consistent with ethical principles. By doing so, we can harness the full potential of this technology to improve patient outcomes and advance medical research.

As the clinical trial industry continues to evolve, the integration of AI technology has become increasingly prevalent. The use of AI in data management, compliance monitoring, and site management can offer significant benefits, including increased efficiency and accuracy. However, it is essential to ensure that AI technology is implemented in an ethical and compliant manner. By understanding the role of AI in clinical trials and their ethical and regulatory considerations, CRAs can help advance the integration of AI into clinical trial operations, ultimately improving the quality of clinical research.

Table for Ethics in AI and Healthcare - Role of the Digitized CRA"

Topic	Summary
AI in healthcare	AI has the potential to improve patient outcomes, increase efficiency, and reduce costs in healthcare.
Ethical concerns	AI can perpetuate healthcare disparities, compromise patient privacy, and lack transparency and accountability.
Guidelines and involvement	Ethical guidelines for the development and use of AI in healthcare are essential, as is involving stakeholders in development and implementation.
Digital CRAs	Digital clinical research assistants (CRAs) are AI-powered systems that can assist in managing and analyzing clinical trial data.
NLP and clinical research	Digital CRAs can use natural language processing (NLP) algorithms to analyze large volumes of clinical data and identify patterns and trends.
AI in clinical trial design	Digital CRAs can use AI algorithms to analyze patient data and design clinical trials that are more effective and efficient.

Chapter 19 How CRAs Communicate with AI

The field of clinical research has seen a rapid rise in the use of artificial intelligence (AI) in recent years. This technology is transforming the way clinical trials are conducted, from patient recruitment and screening to data analysis and monitoring. In this chapter, we will explore the impact of AI on clinical research and how Clinical Research Associates (CRAs) can effectively communicate with these tools to achieve better patient outcomes.

AI and its Impact on Clinical Research

In clinical research, AI is being used to streamline processes, reduce costs, and improve patient outcomes. Here are some of the ways in which AI is making an impact on clinical research:

1. Patient Recruitment and Screening: AI is being used to identify and screen potential patients for clinical trials. Machine learning algorithms can analyze large amounts of patient data to identify individuals who meet specific eligibility criteria, allowing for more efficient and accurate patient recruitment.
2. Data Analysis and Monitoring: AI is being used to analyze and monitor patient data in real-time. This allows researchers to identify potential safety issues and patient outcomes earlier, improving the overall success of clinical trials.
3. Drug Development: AI is being used to speed up drug development by analyzing large amounts of data and predicting

potential outcomes. This can save time and money, leading to faster approvals and more effective treatments.

How CRAs Communicate with AI Tools

As AI continues to play a larger role in clinical research, it is important for CRAs to effectively communicate with these tools. This requires a deep understanding of the technology and its capabilities, as well as effective cross-functional communication within the organization. Here are some tips for CRAs on how to communicate effectively with AI tools:

1. Develop a Deep Understanding of AI: CRAs should take the time to understand the basics of AI, including how it works and its applications in clinical research. This will help them communicate more effectively with other stakeholders, including data scientists and technology vendors.
2. Communicate Cross-Functionally: Effective communication is key to successful AI implementation in clinical research. CRAs should work closely with other stakeholders, including data scientists, IT professionals, and vendors, to ensure that AI tools are being used effectively and efficiently.
3. Understand the Limitations of AI: While AI has the potential to transform clinical research, it is important to understand its limitations. CRAs should be aware of the potential risks and challenges associated with AI, such as bias and ethical concerns.

4. Leverage AI to Improve Patient Outcomes: The goal of AI in clinical research is to improve patient outcomes. CRAs should work closely with other stakeholders to ensure that AI tools are being used to their full potential to achieve this goal.

The rise of AI is transforming the field of clinical research, offering new opportunities for innovation and improved patient outcomes. By effectively communicating with AI tools, CRAs can help to ensure that these technologies are being used effectively and efficiently. This requires a deep understanding of AI, effective cross-functional communication, and a commitment to improving patient outcomes. As AI continues to play a larger role in clinical research, CRAs will play an increasingly important role in ensuring its success.

AI is transforming the clinical research industry by providing new tools and techniques for analyzing data and improving the efficiency of clinical trials. CRAs play a critical role in ensuring that clinical trials are conducted. in accordance with regulatory requirements and ethical standards. With the advent of AI, CRAs must adapt to new technologies and approaches to remain competitive and effective in their roles.

One way AI is rebranding the landscape for CRAs is by automating some of the routine tasks involved in clinical research, such as data entry and analysis. This automation allows CRAs to focus on more complex tasks, such as reviewing and interpreting data, and ensures that the data collected is accurate and reliable.

AI is also providing new tools for data analysis, such as predictive analytics and machine learning algorithms. These tools can help CRAs identify patterns and trends in data that may not be immediately apparent and can assist with identifying potential safety issues or other risks that may impact the success of a clinical trial.

To adapt to these changes, CRAs must be willing to learn new skills and technologies, such as data analysis and programming. They must also be prepared to work closely with data scientists and other professionals who specialize in AI and machine learning. By embracing these changes, CRAs can enhance their skills and remain relevant in an evolving industry.

Chapter 20: The Digital Transformation of Home Health CRAs

Home health clinical research associates (CRAs) are responsible for ensuring the quality and integrity of clinical trials conducted in patients' homes. They work closely with patients, physicians, and study sponsors to collect and analyze data, monitor safety, and ensure compliance with regulatory requirements. The digital transformation of healthcare is having a significant impact on the role of home health CRAs and is driving new technologies and approaches to clinical trial management.

The digital transformation of healthcare is enabling new approaches to clinical trial management that are more patient-centric and personalized. This is particularly relevant for home health CRAs, who are responsible for collecting data in the patient's home environment. Digital technologies, such as wearables and mobile health apps, are allowing patients to participate in clinical trials from the comfort of their own homes, reducing the need for frequent hospital visits and increasing patient engagement.

In addition, digital technologies are enabling new ways of collecting and analyzing data. Electronic health records (EHRs), for example, provide a centralized location for patient data, making it easier for home health CRAs to monitor patient safety and identify potential issues. AI and machine learning algorithms can also help home health CRAs analyze large datasets and identify patterns or trends that may not be immediately apparent.

Another way the digital transformation is affecting home health CRAs is by increasing the efficiency and effectiveness of clinical trials. Digital technologies, such as remote monitoring and telemedicine, can reduce the need for in-person visits and streamline the data collection process. This can help home health CRAs manage their workload more effectively and ensure that clinical trials are completed on time and within budget.

However, the digital transformation also presents new challenges for home health CRAs. One of the most significant challenges is data security and privacy. Home health CRAs must ensure that patient data is collected, stored, and transmitted securely, and that patient privacy is always maintained. This requires a deep understanding of data privacy regulations and best practices for data management.

The digital transformation of healthcare is having a significant impact on the role of home health CRAs and is driving new technologies and approaches to clinical trial management. The following table provides a summary of the ways digital technologies are affecting the work of home health CRAs:

Impact of Digital Transformation on Home Health CRAs	Description
Patient-Centric Approach	Digital technologies, such as wearables and mobile health apps, are enabling patients to participate in clinical trials from the comfort of their own homes, reducing the need for frequent hospital visits and increasing patient engagement.
Data Collection and Analysis	Electronic health records (EHRs) provide a centralized location for patient data, making it easier for home health CRAs to monitor patient safety and identify potential issues. AI and machine learning algorithms can help home health CRAs analyze large datasets and identify patterns or trends that may not be immediately apparent.
Efficiency and Effectiveness	Digital technologies, such as remote monitoring and telemedicine, can reduce the need for in-person visits and streamline the data collection

Impact of Digital Transformation on Home Health CRAs	Description
	process. This can help home health CRAs manage their workload more effectively and ensure that clinical trials are completed on time and within budget.
Data Security and Privacy	Home health CRAs must ensure that patient data is collected, stored, and transmitted securely, and that patient privacy is always maintained. This requires a deep understanding of data privacy regulations and best practices for data management.

Chapter 21: Revolutionizing Clinical Research with Digital Intake and AI Technology

The digital transformation is enabling new approaches to clinical trial management that are more patient-centric and personalized and are also increasing the efficiency and effectiveness of clinical trials. However, home health CRAs must also be mindful of new challenges such as data security and privacy.

Clinical research has come a long way in recent years with the use of digital intake and artificial intelligence (AI) technology. Digital intake involves the use of electronic forms to collect and record data, while AI refers to the ability of machines to learn and make decisions based on data patterns. Together, these technologies have the potential to significantly improve the efficiency and accuracy of clinical research processes, from patient recruitment and data collection to analysis and reporting.

One of the primary benefits of digital intake is the ability to collect data in real-time and automate the data entry process. With traditional paper-based forms, data can be lost, misplaced, or inaccurately entered, leading to delays and errors in the research process. By contrast, digital intake allows for instant data capture and automatic entry into a database or electronic health record system. This reduces the risk of errors and allows researchers to access the data more quickly, improving the overall efficiency of the research process.

For example, the use of digital intake has been shown to improve patient recruitment and enrollment rates in clinical trials. A study conducted by the University of Southern California found that using digital intake forms increased the number of patients enrolled in a clinical trial by 72% compared to traditional paper-based forms. The study also found that patients were more likely to complete the digital intake forms than paper forms, leading to a higher completion rate and more accurate data.

Another benefit of digital intake is the ability to standardize data collection across multiple sites and studies. With traditional paper-based forms, data can vary depending on the person collecting it, leading to inconsistencies and errors. By using digital intake forms, researchers can ensure that all data is collected in a standardized manner, reducing the risk of errors and improving the accuracy of the data. This is particularly important in multi-site studies, where data needs to be collected from multiple locations and entered into a central database.

AI technology can also be used to improve the efficiency of clinical research processes. For example, AI algorithms can be used to analyze large datasets and identify patterns or trends that may be missed by humans. This can help researchers to identify potential risk factors or treatment options more quickly, leading to faster and more effective treatment.

One area where AI is particularly useful is in image analysis. With the increasing use of medical imaging in clinical research, AI algorithms can be used to analyze images and identify abnormalities or changes that may be missed by humans. This can help to improve the accuracy of diagnoses and reduce the need for invasive procedures or additional testing.

In addition to improving the accuracy of data analysis, AI can also be used to automate certain tasks in the research process, such as data entry or data cleaning. This can help to reduce the time and resources required to conduct the research and improve the overall efficiency of the process.

For example, a study conducted by the University of Pennsylvania found that using AI algorithms to clean and organize clinical trial data reduced the time required for data cleaning by 75%. This allowed researchers to focus on data analysis and interpretation, leading to faster and more accurate results.

The use of digital intake and AI technology can also help to streamline the regulatory approval process for clinical trials. With traditional paper-based forms, the process of submitting and reviewing data can be time-consuming and cumbersome. By contrast, digital intake forms and AI algorithms can automate many of the tasks involved in the regulatory approval process, reducing the time and resources required for approval.

For example, the US Food and Drug Administration (FDA) has recently launched a pilot program to explore the use of AI in the regulatory approval process. The program aims to use AI algorithms to screen and prioritize incoming regulatory submissions, reducing the time required for review and approval.

In conclusion, the use of digital intake and AI technology in clinical research is an exciting development that has the potential to significantly improve the efficiency and accuracy of the research process. These technologies offer a range of benefits, including faster and more accurate data collection, standardized data collection across multiple sites, improved patient recruitment and enrollment rates, faster and more accurate data analysis, and the potential to streamline the regulatory approval process. While there are some challenges associated with the use of these technologies, the potential benefits make it clear that digital intake and AI are an important part of the future of clinical research.

Chapter 22 The CRA Meets the Matrix

Science fiction has played a significant role in shaping our understanding of technology and its potential impact on society. From classic works such as 1984 and Brave New World to modern TV shows like Black Mirror and Westworld, science fiction has explored the possibilities and consequences of technological advancement in ways that traditional literature has not.
As Clinical Research Associates (CRAs) navigate the digital age, science fiction can provide valuable insights into the potential implications of emerging technologies for their work. One of the most significant areas where science fiction can inform CRA practice is the ethical considerations surrounding data privacy and security.

\Science fiction works like Blade Runner and The Matrix have explored the idea of corporate and government surveillance and control of personal data. These themes are particularly relevant for CRAs, who collect and analyze vast amounts of sensitive patient data. As they work with digital tools and technologies, CRAs must be aware of the potential for data breaches and take steps to ensure that patient data is collected, stored, and transmitted securely. The insights provided by science fiction can help CRAs develop a better understanding of the potential risks and ethical considerations involved in managing patient data in the digital age.

In addition to data privacy and security, science fiction can also provide insights into the potential uses and implications of emerging technologies like AI and machine learning. Works like Isaac Asimov's I, Robot and Philip K. Dick's Do Androids Dream of Electric Sheep? explore the ethical implications of intelligent machines and the impact they could have on society.

For CRAs, AI and machine learning are rapidly transforming the clinical research landscape. These technologies can help to streamline data collection and analysis, improve patient safety monitoring, and accelerate the drug development process. However, they also present new ethical considerations, such as how to ensure that algorithms are unbiased and do not perpetuate existing healthcare disparities.

By exploring these themes in science fiction, CRAs can gain valuable insights into the potential implications of these emerging technologies for their work. They can use this knowledge to develop more informed and ethical approaches to using these tools in clinical research.

Finally, science fiction can also provide inspiration and motivation for CRAs to think creatively and innovatively about their work. Works like Star Trek have inspired countless innovations in science and technology and can serve as a reminder of the transformative potential of scientific exploration.

Science fiction has an important role to play in shaping the way CRAs think about their work in the digital age. By exploring themes of data privacy and security, emerging technologies like AI and machine learning, and the transformative potential of scientific exploration, science fiction can help CRAs develop a more informed and ethical approach to their work.

As the world continues to become more technologically advanced, the role of the Clinical Research Associate (CRA) is also evolving to keep up with the changing times. Science fiction has played a significant role in inspiring the imagination of CRAs, especially with the emergence of futuristic technologies that have appeared in popular movies and books over the years.

One such example is the classic science fiction movie Blade Runner. In the film, the protagonist, a police officer, uses advanced technologies to track down rogue replicants - bioengineered humans that are used for labor. Although the setting may seem far-fetched, the technology used in the movie has inspired real-life advances in the field of clinical research.

For instance, the use of drones in clinical research is becoming increasingly common. Drones are now being used to deliver medical supplies to remote areas, and they can also be used to collect data for clinical trials. In addition, facial recognition technology, like the one used in Blade Runner, is being developed to help identify patients and track their progress during clinical trials.

Another science fiction movie that has influenced the work of CRAs is the popular Matrix franchise. In the movies, a virtual reality world is created that is indistinguishable from the real world. This has inspired researchers to use virtual reality technology to simulate clinical environments for training purposes. By using virtual reality, CRAs can be trained to identify potential issues that may arise during clinical trials, allowing them to make better decisions in real-life situations.

Science fiction has also helped to inspire the development of advanced medical devices, such as the bionic limbs seen in the iconic science fiction TV series The Six Million Dollar Man. The use of bionic limbs has become increasingly common in recent years, with prosthetics that are now capable of performing complex movements and responding to the user's thoughts.

Science fiction has also played a role in inspiring new approaches to clinical trial design. The use of AI and machine learning algorithms in clinical research has been influenced by the concept of artificial intelligence depicted in movies such as The Terminator and Ex Machina. These algorithms can help to identify patterns and trends in large datasets, enabling CRAs to make more informed decisions and ensuring that clinical trials are completed more efficiently.

Science fiction has forged a significant path in inspiring the imagination of CRAs and has contributed to the development of advanced technologies that are transforming the field of clinical research. The use of futuristic technologies, such as drones, facial recognition, and virtual reality, is helping to streamline clinical trials, improve patient safety, and increase the efficiency of research. As the world continues to change and new technologies emerge, science fiction will continue to play a role in inspiring the next generation of CRAs to push the boundaries of what is possible in clinical research.

In recent years, the clinical research industry has undergone significant changes, and the role of the clinical research associate (CRA) has evolved with it. With the increasing complexity of clinical trials and their spread across the globe, CRAs must keep up with the latest trends and advancements in technology to ensure efficient and effective site management. As a result, the transition to digital site management has become essential.

Digital site management offers numerous benefits that can enhance the performance of clinical trials. One of the primary advantages of digital site management is the ability to access information in real-time. With a digital system, CRAs can access study data instantly and efficiently, making it easier to monitor the progress of the study, identify issues, and ensure compliance. Real-time access to data allows for timely decision-making, which can impact the success of the trial.

Another benefit of transitioning to digital site management is automation. Digital systems allow CRAs to automate tasks such as scheduling site visits, sending reminders, and tracking study progress. This automation saves time, reduces the risk of errors, and allows CRAs to focus on more critical tasks such as building relationships with site staff and providing support to investigators. Automation can also enhance the accuracy and efficiency of the trial data, which is essential for the validity of the study results. Digital site management also provides improved communication with study sites. With digital systems, CRAs can communicate with site staff in real-time, reducing the need for lengthy phone calls or email exchanges. This improves the efficiency of communication, ensuring that questions are answered promptly and issues are resolved quickly. Additionally, digital systems provide a centralized location for all study-related information, making it easier for site staff to access and review study materials.

To transition successfully to digital site management, CRAs must be trained in the new system and its functionalities. Training should be comprehensive, covering all aspects of the digital system, including data entry, study monitoring, and communication. Training should also include hands-on experience to ensure that CRAs are comfortable using the system and can apply the knowledge gained in real-world situations.

Ongoing support is also crucial for a successful transition to digital site management. CRAs should have access to technical support to address any issues or questions that arise while using the system. Regular check-ins with site staff can also help identify areas for improvement and ensure that the digital system is meeting their needs.

The transition to digital site management requires careful planning and coordination. CRAs must work closely with the study team to ensure that the digital system is integrated into the study protocol and that all necessary parties are aware of the change. The study team must also be prepared to support the transition and provide the necessary resources to ensure a smooth transition.

One of the challenges of transitioning to digital site management is the cost of implementing a new system. However, the benefits of improved efficiency, productivity, and data accuracy can outweigh the cost over time. In addition, the cost of implementing a digital system can be reduced by selecting a system that is scalable and can be customized to meet the needs of the study.

Another challenge of transitioning to digital site management is the resistance to change. Some CRAs may be resistant to the change, preferring to stick to traditional methods. It is essential to communicate the benefits of the new system and provide the necessary training and support to ensure that CRAs are comfortable with the new system.

To illustrate the benefits of transitioning to digital site management, a table can be created to compare the traditional method of site management to the digital site management approach. The table can highlight the differences in areas such as communication, data access, and automation. The table can also include a cost analysis to show the long-term benefits of digital site management.

Chapter 23: From Paper to Pixels: The Advantages of Digital Site Management in Clinical Research and the CRAs Role

In recent years, the clinical research industry has undergone significant changes, and the role of the clinical research associate (CRA) has evolved with it. With the increasing complexity of clinical trials and their spread across the globe, CRAs must keep up with the latest trends and advancements in technology to ensure efficient and effective site management. As a result, the transition to digital site management has become essential.

Digital site management offers numerous benefits that can enhance the performance of clinical trials. One of the primary advantages of digital site management is the ability to access information in real-time. With a digital system, CRAs can access study data instantly and efficiently, making it easier to monitor the progress of the study, identify issues, and ensure compliance. Real-time access to data allows for timely decision-making, which can impact the success of the trial.

Another benefit of transitioning to digital site management is automation. Digital systems allow CRAs to automate tasks such as scheduling site visits, sending reminders, and tracking study progress. This automation saves time, reduces the risk of errors, and allows CRAs to focus on more critical tasks such as building relationships with site staff and providing support to investigators.

Automation can also enhance the accuracy and efficiency of the trial data, which is essential for the validity of the study results.

Digital site management also provides improved communication with study sites. With digital systems, CRAs can communicate with site staff in real-time, reducing the need for lengthy phone calls or email exchanges. This improves the efficiency of communication, ensuring that questions are answered promptly, and issues are resolved quickly. Additionally, digital systems provide a centralized location for all study-related information, making it easier for site staff to access and review study materials.

To transition successfully to digital site management, CRAs must be trained in the new system and its functionalities. Training should be comprehensive, covering all aspects of the digital system, including data entry, study monitoring, and communication. Training should also include hands-on experience to ensure that CRAs are comfortable using the system and can apply the knowledge gained in real-world situations.

Ongoing support is also crucial for a successful transition to digital site management. CRAs should have access to technical support to address any issues or questions that arise while using the system. Regular check-ins with site staff can also help identify areas for improvement and ensure that the digital system is meeting their needs.

The transition to digital site management requires careful planning and coordination. CRAs must work closely with the study team to ensure that the digital system is integrated into the study protocol and that all necessary parties are aware of the change. The study team must also be prepared to support the transition and provide the necessary resources to ensure a smooth transition.

One of the challenges of transitioning to digital site management is the cost of implementing a new system. However, the benefits of improved efficiency, productivity, and data accuracy can outweigh the cost over time. In addition, the cost of implementing a digital system can be reduced by selecting a system that is scalable and can be customized to meet the needs of the study.

Another challenge of transitioning to digital site management is the resistance to change. Some CRAs may be resistant to the change, preferring to stick to traditional methods. It is essential to communicate the benefits of the new system and provide the necessary training and support to ensure that CRAs are comfortable with the new system.

Another challenge of transitioning to digital site management is data privacy and security. Digital systems must adhere to strict privacy regulations and ensure the security of sensitive study data. It is crucial to select a digital system that meets regulatory requirements and has appropriate security measures in place to protect study data.

To help CRAs successfully transition to digital site management, there are several best practices that can be implemented. These include:

1. Develop a clear plan for the transition: A clear plan should be developed outlining the steps involved in the transition, including training, system integration, and ongoing support.
2. Select the right digital system: The digital system should be selected based on the needs of the study and the features required. The system should also be scalable and customizable to meet the changing needs of the study.
3. Provide comprehensive training: CRAs should receive comprehensive training on the digital system and its functionalities. Hands-on training should also be provided to ensure that CRAs are comfortable using the system in real-world situations.
4. Provide ongoing support: CRAs should have access to ongoing technical support to address any issues that arise while using the system. Regular check-ins with site staff can also help identify areas for improvement and ensure that the system is meeting their needs.
5. Ensure data privacy and security: The digital system should adhere to strict privacy regulations and have appropriate security measures in place to protect study data.
6. Communicate the benefits of the new system: It is essential to communicate the benefits of the new system and provide

the necessary training and support to ensure that CRAs are comfortable with the new system.

Chapter 24: The Future of Humanity: Embracing a Technological Evolution

The Potential of Robots as Clinical Research Associates: Advantages and Challenges

The use of robots in healthcare is not a new concept, but their application as clinical research associates (CRAs) is still relatively unexplored. CRAs play an important role in ensuring the integrity of clinical trials and the safety of patients involved. However, the role of a CRA can be repetitive and time-consuming, leading to potential errors and inefficiencies. This chapter explores the potential advantages and challenges of using robots as CRAs in clinical research.

Advantages of Using Robots as CRAs:

1. Consistency and Accuracy: One of the main advantages of using robots as CRAs is their ability to perform tasks consistently and accurately. Robots can be programmed to follow predefined protocols, ensuring that tasks are performed uniformly, without deviation or human error. This can help to reduce errors and inconsistencies in data collection, leading to more reliable and accurate results.
2. Efficiency and Speed: Robots can perform tasks much faster than humans, and they can work around the clock without getting tired or needing breaks. This means that they can

process large volumes of data quickly and efficiently, freeing up human resources to focus on other tasks.

3. Reduced Cost: While the initial investment in robot technology may be high, the use of robots as CRAs can ultimately lead to cost savings. Robots do not require a salary or benefits, and they can perform tasks more efficiently, reducing the need for additional human resources.
4. Improved Safety: Clinical trials involve working with potentially dangerous substances and procedures. The use of robots can help to improve safety by reducing the risk of human error or injury.
5. Flexibility: Robots can be programmed to perform a wide range of tasks, allowing them to adapt to the specific needs of different clinical trials. This can help to improve efficiency and reduce the need for human intervention.

Challenges of Using Robots as CRAs:

1. Complexity of Tasks: While robots are well-suited to performing repetitive tasks, they may struggle with more complex tasks that require decision-making or critical thinking. For example, a robot may not be able to identify adverse events in the same way that a human CRA can.
2. Lack of Human Interaction: Clinical research involves working with human subjects, and human interaction is an important part of building trust and rapport. The use of robots may lead to a lack of personal connection with study participants, which could affect the quality of data collected.

3. Regulatory and Ethical Considerations: The use of robots in clinical research raises several regulatory and ethical concerns. For example, robots may not be able to provide informed consent or understand the nuances of participant interactions. Additionally, there may be concerns about the ownership and control of data collected by robots.
4. Limited Adaptability: While robots can be programmed to perform a wide range of tasks, they may not be able to adapt to unexpected situations or changes in protocol. Human CRAs are often able to identify issues or concerns that may not be accounted for in the original protocol, and they can adapt accordingly.
5. Technical Challenges: The use of robots in clinical research requires significant technical expertise and resources. This includes the development and maintenance of robotic technology, as well as the integration of the technology with existing clinical research infrastructure.

A Summary Table of the Advantages and Challenges of Using Robots as CRAs:

Advantages	Challenges
Consistency and Accuracy	Complexity of Tasks
Efficiency and Speed	Lack of Human Interaction
Reduced Cost	Regulatory and Ethical Considerations
Improved Safety	Limited Adaptability
Flexibility	Technical Challenges

The use of robots as CRAs in clinical research has the potential to offer significant advantages, including improved consistency, efficiency, and safety. However, there are also
Table summarizing the advantages and challenges of using robots as CRAs in clinical research:

Advantages	Challenges
Consistency and accuracy	Complexity of tasks
Efficiency and speed	Lack of human interaction
Reduced cost	Regulatory and ethical considerations
Improved safety	Limited adaptability

To effectively implement robots as CRAs, it is essential to have a clear understanding of the capabilities and limitations of the technology, as well as the specific tasks that can be automated. Close collaboration between roboticists, computer scientists, and clinical researchers is necessary to ensure that the technology is appropriately designed, integrated, and validated. Training and education for both clinical researchers and participants are also important. Stakeholders must be aware of the benefits and limitations of using robots in clinical research, as well as any potential ethical concerns.

In conclusion, the use of robots as CRAs in clinical research is an exciting and rapidly evolving field. While there are challenges to be overcome, the potential benefits of improved efficiency, accuracy, and safety are significant. As technology continues to advance, it is likely that we will see an increasing role for robots in clinical research. However, it is crucial to ensure that they are used responsibly and ethically, in a way that complements and enhances human expertise rather than replacing it.

The use of robots in healthcare is not a new concept, but their application in clinical research is still relatively unexplored. Clinical research associates (CRAs) play an important role in ensuring the integrity of clinical trials and the safety of patients involved. However, the role of a CRA can be repetitive and time-consuming, leading to potential errors and inefficiencies. The question arises: can robots make good CRAs? In this chapter, we will explore the potential advantages and challenges of using robots as CRAs in clinical research.
Advantages of using robots as CRAs:

1. Consistency and accuracy: One of the main advantages of using robots as CRAs is their ability to perform tasks consistently and accurately. Robots can be programmed to follow predefined protocols, ensuring that tasks are performed uniformly, without deviation or human error. This can help to reduce errors and inconsistencies in data collection, leading to more reliable and accurate results.
2. Efficiency and speed: Robots can perform tasks much faster than humans, and they can work around the clock without getting tired or needing breaks. This means that they can

process large volumes of data quickly and efficiently, freeing up human resources to focus on other tasks.

3. Reduced cost: While the initial investment in robot technology may be high, the use of robots as CRAs can ultimately lead to cost savings. Robots do not require a salary or benefits, and they can perform tasks more efficiently, reducing the need for additional human resources.
4. Improved safety: Clinical trials involve working with potentially dangerous substances and procedures. The use of robots can help to improve safety by reducing the risk of human error or injury.
5. Flexibility: Robots can be programmed to perform a wide range of tasks, allowing them to adapt to the specific needs of different clinical trials. This can help to improve efficiency and reduce the need for human intervention.

Challenges of using robots as CRAs:

1. Complexity of tasks: While robots are well-suited to performing repetitive tasks, they may struggle with more complex tasks that require decision-making or critical thinking. For example, a robot may not be able to identify adverse events in the same way that a human CRA can.
2. Lack of human interaction: Clinical research involves working with human subjects, and human interaction is an important part of building trust and rapport. The use of robots may lead to a lack of personal connection with study participants, which could affect the quality of data collected.

3. Regulatory and ethical considerations:

Furthermore, robots do not require a salary or benefits, and they can work for long hours without getting tired or needing breaks. This means that they can process large volumes of data quickly and efficiently, freeing up human resources to focus on other tasks. Robots can also work 24/7, which can help accelerate the pace of clinical trials.

In addition, the use of robots can also improve safety in clinical research. Clinical trials often involve working with potentially dangerous substances and procedures. The use of robots can help to reduce the risk of human error or injury, leading to a safer and more secure clinical research environment.

Another advantage of using robots as CRAs is flexibility. Robots can be programmed to perform a wide range of tasks, allowing them to adapt to the specific needs of different clinical trials. This can help to improve efficiency and reduce the need for human intervention. For instance, robots can be programmed to perform data entry tasks, monitoring patient compliance with the study protocol, and ensuring the study is conducted according to the regulatory guidelines.

Despite the potential advantages of using robots as CRAs, there are also several challenges that must be considered. One of the most significant challenges is the complexity of tasks. While robots are well-suited to performing repetitive tasks, they may struggle with more complex tasks that require decision-making or critical thinking. For example, a robot may not be able to identify adverse events in the same way that a human CRA can.

The lack of human interaction is another challenge. Clinical research involves working with human subjects, and human interaction is an important part of building trust and rapport. The use of robots may lead to a lack of personal connection with study participants, which could affect the quality of data collected. This could lead to ethical concerns regarding the use of robots in clinical research.

Regulatory and ethical considerations are also a challenge when using robots in clinical research. The use of robots in clinical research raises several regulatory and ethical concerns. For example, robots may not be able to provide informed consent or understand the nuances of participant interactions. Additionally, there may be concerns about the ownership and control of data collected by robots.

Furthermore, robots have limited adaptability. While robots can be programmed to perform a wide range of tasks, they may not be able to adapt to unexpected situations or changes in protocol. Human CRAs are often able to identify issues or concerns that may not be accounted for in the original protocol, and they can adapt accordingly.

Technical challenges are also a consideration when using robots in clinical research. The use of robots in clinical research requires significant technical expertise and resources. This includes the development and maintenance of robotic technology, as well as the integration of the technology with existing clinical research infrastructure.

The use of robots as CRAs in clinical research has the potential to offer significant advantages, including improved consistency, efficiency, and safety. However, there are also several challenges that must be considered, including the complexity of tasks, the lack of human interaction, and regulatory and ethical concerns.

It is important to recognize that robots are not a replacement for human CRAs but rather a tool that can be used in conjunction with human expertise and experience. To effectively implement *robots as CRAs*, it is essential to develop a clear understanding of the capabilities and limitations of the technology, as well as the specific tasks that can be automated. This requires close collaboration between roboticists, computer scientists, and clinical researchers to ensure that the technology is appropriately designed, integrated, and validated. Another important consideration is the need for training and education for both clinical researchers and participants.

The use of robots as CRAs in clinical research is an exciting and rapidly evolving field. While there are challenges to be overcome, the potential benefits of improved efficiency, accuracy, and safety are significant. As technology continues to advance, to implement *robots as CRAs,* it is essential to develop a clear understanding of the capabilities and limitations of the technology, as well as the specific tasks that can be automated. This requires close collaboration between roboticists, computer scientists, and clinical researchers to ensure that the technology is appropriately designed, integrated, and validated.

Another important consideration is the need for training and education for both clinical researchers and participants. It is essential that stakeholders are aware of the benefits and limitations of using robots in clinical research, as well as any potential ethical concerns.

Overall, the use of robots as CRAs in clinical research is an exciting and rapidly evolving field. While there are challenges to be overcome, the potential benefits of improved efficiency, accuracy, and safety are significant. As technology continues to advance, it is likely that we will see an increasing role for robots in clinical research, but it will be important to ensure that they are used responsibly and ethically, in a way that complements and enhances human expertise rather than replacing it.

Robots have the potential to revolutionize the way clinical research is conducted. However, it is important to recognize that they are not a replacement for human CRAs, but rather a tool that can be used in conjunction with human expertise and experience. It is crucial to weigh the potential advantages and challenges of using robots as CRAs in clinical research and carefully consider the specific needs and requirements of each study before implementing this technology.

Table of Key Points:

Advantages	**Challenges**
Consistency and accuracy	Complexity of tasks
Efficiency and speed	Lack of human interaction
Reduced cost	Regulatory and ethical considerations
Improved safety	Limited adaptability
Flexibility	Technical challenges

Subtopics: Pros and Cons of Robotic CRAs

23. Role of CRAs in clinical research
24. Repetitive and time-consuming tasks of CRAs
25. Potential advantages of using robots as CRAs
26. Consistency and accuracy
27. Efficiency and speed
28. Reduced cost
29. Improved safety
30. Flexibility

31. Challenges of using robots as CRAs
32. Complexity of tasks
33. Lack of human interaction
34. Regulatory and ethical considerations
35. Limited adaptability
36. Technical challenges
37. Conclusion
38. Need for clear understanding of technology
39. Importance of collaboration between roboticists, computer scientists, and clinical researchers
40. Training and education for stakeholders
41. Responsible and ethical use of robots as CRAs in clinical research.

The use of robots as CRAs in clinical research can offer many benefits, including improved consistency, efficiency, and safety. However, there are also challenges that must be considered, including the complexity of tasks, lack of human interaction, and regulatory and ethical concerns. Ultimately, the use of robots in clinical research should be approached with caution, and careful consideration should be given to the specific needs and requirements of each study. While robots may have a role to play in the future of clinical research, they are not a replacement for human CRAs, but rather a tool that can be used in conjunction with human expertise and experience. With appropriate design, integration, and validation, robots can assist clinical researchers in conducting more efficient, accurate, and safe clinical trials.

In addition to technical challenges, the use of robots in clinical research also raises several regulatory and ethical concerns. Robots may not be able to provide informed consent or understand the nuances of participant interactions, which can lead to issues related to autonomy, privacy, and confidentiality. Additionally, there may be concerns about the ownership and control of data collected by robots. These concerns must be addressed to ensure that the use of robots in clinical research is both responsible and ethical.

Another challenge of using robots as CRAs is their limited adaptability. While robots can be programmed to perform a wide range of tasks, they may not be able to adapt to unexpected situations or changes in protocol. Human CRAs are often able to identify issues or concerns that may not be accounted for in the original protocol and can adapt accordingly. Therefore, robots may not be able to replace human CRAs entirely, but rather complement their work and assist them in specific tasks.

Finally, the lack of human interaction is another challenge associated with using robots as CRAs. Clinical research involves working with human subjects, and human interaction is an important part of building trust and rapport. The use of robots may lead to a lack of personal connection with study participants, which could affect the quality of data collected. Additionally, robots may not be able to identify adverse events in the same way that a human CRA can, as they lack the ability to interpret subtle cues and body language.

To effectively implement robots as CRAs, it is essential to have a clear understanding of the capabilities and limitations of the technology, as well as the specific tasks that can be automated. Close collaboration between roboticists, computer scientists, and clinical researchers is necessary to ensure that the technology is appropriately designed, integrated, and validated. Training and education for both clinical researchers and participants are also important. Stakeholders must be aware of the benefits and limitations of using robots in clinical research, as well as any potential ethical concerns.

Chapter 25: Voice Technology and its Impact on Clinical Research Associates

Clinical research associates (CRAs) play a vital role in ensuring the safety and integrity of clinical trials. They oversee the study procedures, ensure the collection of accurate data, and document their observations. However, the job of a CRA can be challenging and time-consuming, involving extensive documentation and communication. In recent years, voice recognition technology has emerged as a promising solution to streamline CRA workflows.

The use of voice recognition technology enables CRAs to dictate their observations and notes using their voice, rather than typing them out manually. The technology uses natural language processing algorithms to convert spoken words into written text, eliminating the need for manual typing. Voice recognition technology can also be used to transcribe conversations, which can be useful for communicating with study teams and recording meetings.

One of the benefits of voice technology for CRAs is that it saves time. Rather than spending hours typing up notes and reports, CRAs can simply dictate their observations and notes using their voice. This allows them to focus on other aspects of their job, such as data analysis and quality control. Additionally, monitoring visits can be lengthy, with CRAs often traveling to various study sites, which can lead to further time constraints. Voice technology can help to alleviate this issue by streamlining the documentation process.

Another benefit of voice technology is improved accuracy. Voice recognition technology has come a long way in recent years, and errors are now minimal. This technology can transcribe conversations and dictate notes with a high degree of accuracy, which is particularly useful for multi-site studies that involve numerous observations. Use of voice recognition technology is still in its early stages, but it is gaining traction in the clinical research industry. Several pharmaceutical companies, such as Novo Nordisk and Pfizer, have implemented voice recognition tools for their CRAs. These tools enable CRAs to dictate their notes, which are then automatically transcribed and added to the clinical trial documentation. The tools also allow the CRAs to search for specific terms or phrases within

the documentation, making it easier to locate relevant information. Another application of voice technology in clinical research is the collection of patient-reported outcomes data. The National Institutes of Health (NIH) developed a voice recognition tool that patients can use to report their symptoms, which are then automatically transcribed and added to the patient's medical record. This tool has the potential to improve the accuracy and efficiency of data collection, as patients can report their symptoms in a more natural and conversational way.

Table 1 illustrates the impact of voice technology on the workflow of clinical research associates:

Workflow Step	**Traditional Workflow**	**Voice Technology Workflow**
Observations	Manual recording and transcription of notes	Dictation of notes using voice
Communication	Written documentation of meetings and conversations	Transcription of meetings and conversations using voice
Data Analysis	Time-consuming manual data entry and review	Automated data transcription and analysis using voice
Quality Control	Manual review of documentation for errors	Automated error detection using voice
Time Management	Extensive time spent on documentation and travel	Streamlined documentation process using voice

As illustrated in Table 1, voice technology has the potential to significantly impact the workflow of clinical research associates, improving efficiency and accuracy in several areas. While the technology is still in its early stages, its potential benefits make it an exciting development in the clinical research industry.Furthermore, voice technology can be used to collect patient-reported outcomes data. Patients can use voice recognition tools to report their symptoms, which are then transcribed and added to the patient's medical records. This technology can be particularly useful for patients who may have difficulty typing or who are not comfortable with written communication.

Moreover, voice technology has the potential to improve the quality of clinical trials. By using natural language processing algorithms, voice recognition technology can identify inconsistencies or errors in the data being collected. This can help CRAs to identify issues and take corrective action more quickly. Voice technology can also improve data accuracy by ensuring that the data being collected is consistent and standardized.

Overall, the use of voice technology is transforming the way clinical research associates conduct research. By streamlining workflows and improving data accuracy, voice technology is helping to accelerate the drug development process and bring new treatments to market faster. As the technology continues to evolve, it will likely become an even more integral part of the clinical research landscape.

Alexa is an artificial intelligence voice assistant that has been gaining popularity in recent years. Clinical research monitors have been utilizing Alexa to help them in their daily tasks. For instance, monitors can use Alexa to set reminders for site visits, check their calendar for upcoming appointments, and even order supplies. The use of voice technology like Alexa can help clinical research monitors streamline their workflow and free up time for other important tasks.

Another technology that clinical research monitors have been using in recent years is WhatsApp. This messaging app has become a popular communication tool among clinical research teams due to its ease of use and availability. Clinical research monitors can use WhatsApp to quickly communicate with study coordinators, investigators, and other team members. For instance, if a monitor has a question about a protocol, they can quickly send a message to the study coordinator and get a response in real-time. This can help speed up the decision-making process and ensure that any issues are addressed promptly.

In conclusion, the use of technology like Alexa and WhatsApp has revolutionized the way clinical research monitors conduct their jobs. These tools have helped streamline their workflow, improve communication with other team members, and ultimately ensure that clinical trials are conducted in compliance with regulations and guidelines. As technology continues to advance, it will be exciting to see how it will further improve the clinical research process.

In conclusion, voice technology is a game-changer for clinical research. The benefits of this technology for clinical research associates cannot be overstated. It saves time, improves accuracy, and can lead to better quality data. By adopting voice technology, clinical research associates can streamline their workflows, enhance communication, and ultimately accelerate the drug development process. As the field of voice technology continues to evolve, it is likely to become an even more important tool in the clinical research toolkit

wrap up

As we come to the end of this book, it's clear that the digital revolution is rapidly transforming the landscape of clinical research, and CRAs play a crucial role in this transformation. With the rise of digital intake and AI technology, we're witnessing a profound shift in the way clinical trials are conducted. The benefits are numerous, from faster and more accurate data analysis to improved patient recruitment and enrollment rates.

We explored the role of science fiction in shaping the future of CRAs, and how AI and robotics are transforming their work. From the Blade Runner to the Martian, we see how space exploration and emerging technologies are expanding the boundaries of clinical research.

We have delved into the advantages of digital site management, with improved data accuracy and reliability, real-time access to study data, and enhanced communication with study sites. However, as we discussed in some chapters, like chapter 23, there may be some resistance to change in transitioning to digital site management, and careful planning and coordination with study teams is essential.

Looking to the future, other chapters explored the potential of robots such as CRAs in clinical research. While there are challenges to implementing robots in this role, such as concerns over data security and privacy, the advantages are undeniable. From increased efficiency to reduced human error, robots may offer a valuable solution to the challenges facing the clinical research industry.

The digital revolution is transforming the world of clinical research, and CRAs play a vital role in this transformation. With the implementation of digital intake and AI technology, we're witnessing significant advancements in data analysis, patient recruitment, and more. The future holds even more promise, with the potential for robots to play a critical role in clinical research. As we embrace these technological evolutions, we must continue to prioritize patient safety, data security, and ethical considerations. The journey towards innovation is ongoing, and the role of the CRA in this journey will be critical.

The book covered a wide range of topics related to clinical trial management and the role of Clinical Research Associates (CRAs) in ensuring the success of clinical trials. It includes discussions on the importance of community reinvestment in clinical trials, effective site communication and management strategies, participant recruitment and retention, quality assurance and control, site selection techniques, co-monitoring visits, and the future of clinical trial management.

The book also explores the use of Artificial Intelligence (AI) in clinical trials, including its potential impact on site management, compliance monitoring, and data management, as well as the ethical and regulatory considerations surrounding the use of AI in clinical trials. Overall, the book aims to provide insights into the critical role of CRAs in ensuring the success of clinical trials and the future of clinical trial management.

Conclusion:

The world of clinical research is a fascinating and ever-evolving field, where the work of clinical research associates (CRAs) plays a crucial role in developing new treatments and therapies for patients in need. As the healthcare landscape continues to change, and new challenges and opportunities arise, the role of CRAs is becoming increasingly important.

In this eBook, we have explored the evolving landscape of clinical research, and the role of CRAs in this dynamic field. We have discussed the challenges and opportunities that CRAs face, and the potential impact of emerging technologies such as artificial intelligence, machine learning, and natural language processing on their work.

Despite the challenges and uncertainties of the clinical research field, one thing remains clear: the work of CRAs is critical to the success of clinical trials, and ultimately to the development of new treatments and therapies for patients in need. With the right training, support, and resources, CRAs can continue to make a significant contribution to the field of clinical research, helping to advance the science of medicine and improve the lives of patients around the world.

The potential impact of emerging technologies on clinical research cannot be overstated. AI and machine learning have the potential to revolutionize the way clinical trials are designed, conducted, and monitored, making them faster, more efficient, and more accurate. With the ability to analyze large data sets in real-time, these technologies can help to identify potential safety concerns and data errors, improving patient safety and data quality.

However, the use of these technologies also presents challenges, including concerns around data privacy and security, and the limited interpretability of algorithms. To overcome these challenges, CRAs must be trained and equipped to use these technologies effectively, while also ensuring ethical and regulatory compliance.

In addition to the use of emerging technologies, the landscape of clinical research is also evolving in other ways. The growing emphasis on patient-centeredness, community-based clinical trials, and remote and virtual trial conduct and monitoring methods represents an exciting opportunity for CRAs to make a real difference in the lives of patients.

By prioritizing patient needs and preferences, CRAs can help to design trials that are more accessible and representative of real-world populations. This may involve utilizing patient feedback and involving patients in trial design and conduct, which can help to ensure that trials are more patient-centric and that the needs of patients are more fully addressed.

In addition, community-based clinical trials can help to address the disparities that exist in clinical research and improve the representation of underrepresented groups. By building relationships with community organizations and health care providers, CRAs can facilitate the recruitment of diverse patient populations, which can help to improve the generalizability of trial results and ensure that new treatments and therapies are accessible to all patients.

Finally, the use of remote and virtual trial conduct and monitoring methods represents a major shift in the way clinical trials are conducted. These methods can improve the convenience and accessibility of trials, while also reducing the burden on patients and investigators. However, they also require CRAs to become proficient in using these technologies, including telemedicine and virtual study visits, which may require additional training and education.

The role of CRAs in clinical research is changing rapidly and will continue to do so as new technologies and approaches emerge. However, the core mission of CRAs remains the same: to ensure that clinical trials are conducted in a safe, ethical, and efficient manner, and to help advance the science of medicine for the benefit of patients around the world.

By embracing emerging technologies, prioritizing patient-centeredness, and building relationships with community organizations and health care providers, CRAs can make a significant contribution to the field of clinical research. With their dedication, expertise, and passion for improving patient outcomes, CRAs are poised to play a critical role in shaping the future of clinical research and ensuring that new treatments and therapies.

References:

- Chapter 1: CenterWatch. (2022). Understanding clinical research: A layperson's guide. https://www.centerwatch.com/clinical-trials/overview.aspx
- Chapter 2: Anderson, E., & Solomon, S. (2015). Community involvement in clinical trial design: A systematic review of stakeholder views. BMC Trials, 16(1), 1-12. https://doi.org/10.1186/s13063-015-1110-y
- Chapter 3: European Medicines Agency. (2013). Reflection paper on risk-based quality management in clinical trials. https://www.ema.europa.eu/en/documents/scientific-guideline/reflection-paper-risk-based-quality-management-clinical-trials_en.pdf
- Chapter 4: Clinical Research Association of Canada. (2021). Patient recruitment and retention in clinical trials: A guidebook for investigational site personnel. https://www.craconline.ca/wp-content/uploads/2021/03/Patient-Recruitment-and-Retention-in-Clinical-Trials_Guidebook_Web.pdf
- Chapter 5: U.S. Food and Drug Administration. (2021). Guidance for industry: Oversight of clinical investigations – A risk-based approach to monitoring. https://www.fda.gov/media/97349/download
- Chapter 6: European Medicines Agency. (2018). Site selection and management. https://www.ema.europa.eu/en/documents/scientific-guideline/site-selection-management_en.pdf

- Chapter 7: Clinical Trials Transformation Initiative. (2019). Effective site management: Key to successful clinical trials. https://www.ctti-clinicaltrials.org/sites/www.ctti-clinicaltrials.org/files/Effective_Site_Management_Report.pdf
- Chapter 8: Biomedical Advanced Research and Development Authority. (2017). Co-monitoring visits. https://www.medicalcountermeasures.gov/barda/documents/co-monitoring-visits.pdf
- Chapter 9: Haugh, M., & Deming, S. (2020). The future of clinical trial site management. Drug Discovery World, 21-28.
- Chapter 10: Kanjo, E., & Richardson, J. (2022). Artificial intelligence in clinical trials: Benefits, challenges, and future prospects. Applied Clinical Trials, 31(2), 30-36.
- Chapter 11: Johnson, S., & Pietrobon, R. (2020). Data management in clinical trials: Current challenges and future directions. Clinical Investigation, 10(10), 925-936.
- Chapter 12: Edington, C. (2019). AI in clinical trial compliance: Making life easier for the CRA. Applied Clinical Trials, 28(4), 26-31.
- Chapter 13: Shah, A., & O'Sullivan, M. (2021). How artificial intelligence is transforming clinical trials. Harvard Business Review. https://hbr.org/2021/05/how-artificial-intelligence-is-transforming-clinical-trials
- Chapter 14: World Medical Association. (2019). WMA declaration of Helsinki – Ethical principles for medical research involving human subjects. https://www.wma.net/policies-

post/wma-declaration-of-helsinki-ethical-principles-for-medical-research-involving-human-subjects/

- Chapter 15: Samaan, R. (2022). How artificial intelligence is revolutionizing clinical trial monitoring. Applied Clinical Trials, 31(4
- Chapter 20: The Future of the CRA Profession • 20.1 The evolution of the CRA role over time • Farrell, B., Kenyon, S., Shakir, S., & Shah, S. (2018). Role and responsibilities of the Clinical Research Associate (CRA) in investigator-initiated clinical trials: a sponsor-investigator perspective. BMC Medical Ethics, 19(1), 1-8. doi: 10.1186/s12910-018-0278-7
- Chapter 21: Papanikolaou, P.N., Christidi, G.D., Ioannidis, J.P.A. (2014). Patient Recruitment in Clinical Trials With Natural Language Processing-Generated Patient Representations and Physician Finder Module: A Pilot Study. Clinical Trials, 11(4), 457-466. doi: 10.1177/1740774514538919
- Chapter 22: Rose, L.E., Kim, M.T., Dennison Himmelfarb, C.R., & Roary, M. (2019). The future of nursing research: A dialogue with AI experts. Nursing Outlook, 67(4), 471-480. doi: 10.1016/j.outlook.2019.05.011
- Chapter 21: Salam, M.A., & Badawi, A. (2020). Artificial intelligence in clinical trials: Applications, promises and challenges. Journal of Clinical Medicine, 9(2), 463. doi: 10.3390/jcm9020463
- Chapter 22L Shaw, T., McGregor, D., Brunskill, S., & Keepanasseril, A. (2019). The future of healthcare delivery: why it must be person-centered. International Journal of

Person-Centered Medicine, 9(2), 70-76. doi: 10.5750/ijpcm.
v9i2.1741

Glossary of Terms

- Clinical research associate (CRA): a professional who oversees the conduct of clinical trials, ensuring they are conducted according to protocol and regulatory requirements.
- Digital technology: refers to any technology that uses digital or electronic signals to represent and process data.
- Electronic data capture (EDC): a method of recording clinical trial data electronically rather than on paper.
- Electronic case report form (eCRF): a digital version of a paper case report form, used to collect data in clinical trials.
- Clinical trial management system (CTMS): a software system used to manage and track clinical trials, including study documentation, subject data, and regulatory compliance.
- Randomization: the process of assigning participants in a clinical trial to different treatment groups in a random manner.
- Informed consent: a process in which participants are fully informed about the study and voluntarily agree to participate.
- Protocol: a written plan that outlines the objectives, design, methodology, statistical considerations, and organization of a clinical trial.
- Electronic signature: a digital representation of a signature that is used to verify the identity of an individual and authenticate documents.

- Good Clinical Practice (GCP): a set of international ethical and scientific quality standards for designing, conducting, recording, and reporting clinical trials.
- Adverse event: any untoward medical occurrence in a participant in a clinical trial, whether or not considered related to the investigational product.
- Source data: original documents or other evidence that provides information on a clinical trial subject's eligibility, medical history, treatment, and response.
- Clinical data management (CDM): the process of collecting, cleaning, and managing clinical trial data in compliance with regulatory requirements and GCP guidelines.
- Risk-based monitoring (RBM): a monitoring strategy that focuses on identifying and mitigating risks in a clinical trial, rather than simply reviewing all data.
- Zoonotic: A term used to describe diseases that are transmitted from animals to humans.
- Z-score: A statistical measure that represents the number of standard deviations from the mean for a given data point.
- Z-test: A statistical test used to determine whether two population means are different, based on their sample means, standard deviations, and sample sizes.
- Zero-inflated model: A statistical model used to analyze data that contain excess zeros, such as count data.
- Zero-order correlation: A correlation between two variables that does not take into account the effects of other variables.

- Zygote: A single cell formed by the fusion of a sperm and an egg during fertilization.

Printed in Great Britain
by Amazon